"…a gay *Desperate Housewives*."

"You'll never look at suburbia in the sa
and racier *Tales of the City*, crossed v ̱ ̱ Burroughs' first
novel *Sellevision* with a good dose of *Desperate Housewives* thrown
in… it's full of life and laughs… Arvin handles the action like a
maestro, his prose is fun and light, a complete pleasure to read, and it
seems like only a matter of time until *SubSurdity* makes it to a screen
near you."

—Charlotte Cooper, Gaydarnation

"Anyone wise enough to purchase [*SubSurdity*] will most certainly
enjoy the ride!"

—J.L. Foster, author of *Straight*

"The perfect summer read—it's light, it's fun, and it will keep you
reading. In fact, I have not had this much fun in a long time… this book
should be at the top of your must-read list."

—Amos Lassen, Literary Pride

"Like *Knots Landing* crossing *Tales of the City*, this book is a winner in
that it puts a humorous spin on the stories of its characters and the
bubbly adventures in their lives. *The Rest is Illusion* was a wonderfully
auspicious debut… and *SubSurdity* gives us a peek at why [Arvin is]
here for the long haul."

—Carey Parrish, webdigestweekly.com

"Written with a crisp humorous dialogue that will at times make you
laugh out loud you can easily get lost in the antics of these wacky
neighbors."

—Nick Strathern, TLA Books

By ERIC ARVIN

Another Enchanted April
Galley Proof
Simple Men
Woke Up in a Strange Place

SubSurdity
Suburbilicious
SuburbaNights

Slight Details and Random Events

Kid Christmas Rides Again

Published by DREAMSPINNER PRESS
http://www.dreamspinnerpress.com

SuburbaNights

Eric Arvin

vignettes from Jasper Lane

Dreamspinner Press

Published by
Dreamspinner Press
382 NE 191st Street #88329
Miami, FL 33179-3899, USA
http://www.dreamspinnerpress.com/

Cover Art by Charles Esquiaqui A quixer@gmail.com

ISBN: 978-1-61372-597-9

Printed in the United States of America
First Edition
July 2012

eBook edition available
eBook ISBN: 978-1-61372-598-6

For my Aunt Joyce

The Chapter With the Magic Christians

"OH, THAT *Terrence*! I could just wring his neck!"

Melinda Gold paced furiously back and forth on the deck, her hands clenched tight, as Cassie Bloom listened. It was just the pair of them this afternoon at Cassie's magnificent home. It was late October, but a warm, glowing day. Both women were dressed casually and comfortably. Cassie had a pair of white-framed sunglasses perched atop her short golden hair. Melinda wore a trendy blue cashmere top.

"Leave it to Terrence to ruin everything! It had all been so perfect until he showed up. The park was lovely, so quiet and peaceful. Things might have even become romantic if given the chance. My date—you remember Mr. Lintrope?—he and I were sitting by the duck pond in a nice secluded spot away from the jogging paths. The flowers and trees and birds decorated the scene for us. And of course, the meal I made last night for our date today was triumphant, if I do say so."

"Mr. Lintrope?" Cassie interrupted. "The librarian?"

Melinda stopped pacing long enough to give Cassie a warning stare. "Yes, the librarian! There's nothing wrong with librarians. They're *somewhat* respectable, anyway. I think he would have brought some stability back into my life. Not that I'll ever know now. But he would have been good for me. Sure, there were some of his quirks that I didn't care for. We'd definitely need to work on the nose hair issue, but...."

She shook her head, regaining control of her narrative. She pinned a strand of loose hair behind her ear. "I made my barbecue chicken. Everyone loves my barbecue chicken. You remember how well it went

1

over at the Fourth of July party. Mr. Lintrope was just about to take a bite when...."

"Terrence."

"Terrence!" Melinda screamed. "He comes tearing out of the bushes like some carefree heathen, just ripping his clothes off. Just ripping them off and throwing them hither and dither. He didn't even see us. I nearly went epileptic. Mr. Lintrope looked at me and asked, 'Isn't that your friend?' I hadn't the time or the ability to respond, Cassie. Terrence was stark raving naked and playing around in the pond like a three-year-old in bathwater, all giggling and singing. Why does he *always* have to sing? It's like he's a member of that damn *Sound of Music* family. I'd hate to meet the rest of his family, I'll tell you that!" She crossed her arms and tightened her jaw. "It was only then that he saw Mr. Lintrope and me."

"Darling, Mr. Lintrope can't hold you accountable for a friend's quirks." Cassie was enjoying this. She was so wrapped up in the story her afternoon cocktail had hardly been sipped from.

"That's not the end of it. Oh, no. The story continues, Cassie. Oh, does it ever!" Melinda pulled out a chair from the table and sat down with a huff. "Terrence's frolicking and giggling and singing had been so loud it brought the attention of a group of joggers who were on a nearby path. And who do you think those joggers were, Cassie?"

"I have no idea. This is exciting."

"None other than Coach... *Nipple* and his star wrestlers."

Cassie cackled, clapping her knee. "Imagine that!"

"They thought Terrence was drowning and were coming to his rescue. I can't blame them. He definitely sounded like a creature in peril. Well, when he saw them and realized what they were thinking, he played right into it. *The worm!* The wrestlers jumped into the pond, stripping as they dove, and all three of them grabbed hold of our flailing Terrence. When they got him to land, he fainted. He actually fainted... or he pretended to faint so he could be revived. Then he *re-*fainted two more times. All three wrestlers had to give him mouth-to-mouth. And they were all nearly naked, Cassie! Naked!"

Cassie could say nothing. She could barely sit up straight.

"Well, I'm glad someone sees humor in the situation. The coach looked at me, finally taking notice I was there, and gave me a grin. Like the kind he used to give me after we had… you know. Mr. Lintrope *saw* that grin. Any handsome man would be intimidated by the coach's presence. He commands attention. How do you think an average man like Mr. Lintrope felt? After Terrence was dressed and I was left alone again with my date, I asked Mr. Lintrope if we could try this another time, and he said, rather unconvincingly, 'Sure. I'll give you a call.' Can you believe it?" Melinda clenched her fists again. "That Terrence!"

"Indeed. What a treasure," Cassie said. "And he seems to get on your bad side more than anybody I've known."

Melinda sat back in her chair, as if she was relieved to have told her story and now exhausted. Cassie reached across the table for her cell phone. Melinda, of course, knew what was coming.

"You can't even wait a few minutes?" Melinda asked.

"Vera," Cassie said into the phone, "get over here now. Melinda has just been through an ordeal with that dull-as-bones Mr. Lintrope, and it's hilarious."

JUST down the street from Cassie Bloom's place, Terrence—the very troublemaker Melinda was ranting about—reclined fully clothed in a lounge chair on the back patio of the Cooper-Tuckers. James sat opposite him with a laptop over his stretched-out legs. His hair was worn shaggy now and in need of a trim—a far cry from his military days.

"She completely overreacted," Terrence was saying. "It is a beautiful day and I wanted to have a dip, not be harassed by one. What a drama queen."

James, clearly unimpressed with the story Terrence was telling, even with the extravagant hand gestures and likely truth-stretching, shut his laptop, stared up at the sun from beneath his sunglasses, and prayed for deafness. "Shouldn't Rick be the one hearing all of this?" he said. "Shouldn't you wait for him to get home from work and tell *him*?"

"You know, James, I don't ask for much from you. Just an ear to bitch to from time to time when Rick isn't here. Is that too much to ask. Huh? A little respect. The same respect you'd give any stranger on the street!" He sipped his rum and cola dry, then shook the ice in the glass. "I need a refresher."

"Get it yourself."

"Besides," Terrence said as he mixed another drink from the cola and rum on the table, "what do you have to do that's more important than my scintillating conversation? You look at Internet porn all day while Rick is out. That requires your eyes, not your ears."

"It's addictive." James shrugged as he reopened his laptop.

Terrence sat back in the lounge once again. "Yes. I know. Me and Rick have had many a discussion about said Internet porno addiction. If I were the judgmental type—" Sip, sip, sip. "—I would say there might be something amiss in the bedroom land of Cooper-Tucker."

"And who would you say this to? Me?"

"What you need is a hobby."

"Like what? Stamp collecting?"

"Try licking. Stamp licking. And by licking I mean 'my ass.' Jesus, James! Put some thought into it. Find something new to do. You don't want Rick feeling inadequate, do you?"

James at last looked thoughtfully at Terrence. "Why would he feel inadequate?"

"Don't glisten your chesticles at me like that. You know how. Those porn sites are filled with guys who might as well wear three-legged jeans. There are guys on those sites—and I have visited them all, believe you me—there are guys who would qualify as kickstands. I hear there is a porn company in Russia that even genetically alters men on big crazy farms. They grow these huge penises the size of your leg."

James rolled his eyes. "Well, if I need a hobby, so do you. Do you hear the ridiculous shit you're spewing? It's like the plot of some gay science fiction epic."

4

"I have a hobby." Terrence put his drink down defiantly. "I'm getting back into cheerleading."

"You'll break a hip."

"I just need something to cheer for." He raised an eyebrow. "Maybe your rugby team. There's an idea. How would you like that?"

James looked back to his laptop, interest lost. "Sure. Why not? The guys would like that." His tone was neither approving nor sarcastic.

"We'll try not to be too big of a distraction to you."

"What's your son, Christian, been up to? Does he like college?" James continued surfing the net even as he conversed.

"From what I hear, he's ecstatic about the place."

James chuckled. "Who would have thought a son of yours would ever go to Bible college?"

"It's distressing. But he *loves* Jesus, and I love Christian. What else can I do?"

"And Harry? Your big plaid-sportin' church-lovin' manly man. How are things with him?"

Terrence smacked his lips. "We're one big happy Christian family."

"Oh. Speaking of Christians...."

"Must we?"

"I hear tell that the new family who moved into Steve and Sandy's old place is quite devout."

Terrence looked horrified and gave a sneer. "Devout?"

James looked up from his laptop and lowered his sunglasses. "*De-vout.*"

"Dammit," Terrence said. "And just as we've made such good progress with Melinda Gold. Those devout Christians are everywhere! Just like glitter. You can't get rid of them, can you?"

"Something tells me you're going to try."

"Well, of course. That's what I do."

IT WAS a lovely afternoon as Cliff jogged back through the neighborhood. His muscles, pumped and swollen from the intense training regimen he had been putting them through, rose and fell, flexed and undulated as he showed them off, nearly naked under the sun. And why shouldn't he show them off? He would soon be a competitive bodybuilder, after all. Showing off was what they did.

Behind him was his handsome piece of husband, David, driving a golf cart—the same golf cart Patrick Gold had driven into his mother's pool. Melinda had not been pleased. It had been repaired and now ran perfectly again. David had bought it from Patrick for what the boy's thieving grandmother, Nanna Hench, had paid for it. The boy was in college, after all, and needed the cash for nefarious doings.

Cliff was getting used to his new body. The bulking phase—which he had been quite familiar with all of his life—was over, and he was now as cut as he had ever been. He had mentioned to David that he wasn't sure he liked being quite so cut. A swollen muscle body had always appealed more to him than the shredded look. David didn't seem to mind, however, and truth be told, they had fun in bed either way. In fact, today being their anniversary, they planned to have quite a bit of that fun tonight.

They passed a plethora of festive scenery on the jog. The houses in the neighborhood were adorned in their finest Halloween attire. Yes, a favorite collective holiday was approaching. In just over a week, Cassie Bloom would once again be holding a massive Halloween party to rival all others. Her decorations for it had already started going up.

As they rounded the curb back onto Jasper Lane, Cliff slowed to a walk and placed his hands on his hips to take a breather. He was sweating in great drops, not so much a sign of any heat as it was of the intensity with which he trained. David pulled up beside him in the golf cart.

"You okay, baby?" David asked. "Need a drink?" He held out a bottled water.

Cliff looked around, breathing hard. "My stomach is just getting to me."

"You're going to do great. There's no sense in getting nervous this early. You've got months before your first major expo."

"I haven't placed in any of the amateur competitions yet. I'm thinking this one won't be any different."

"Don't talk like that, dummy. You'll jinx yourself. You know what I think it is? I think those judges in the amateurs were jealous of you."

"How do you figure, babe?"

"Look at you. You're a superstar! You had an amazing career in adult film, and you retired on top. Plus, you're the author of a best-selling book."

Cliff smiled and wiped his brow. "A ghostwriter wrote that, babe. I just dictated it."

"But it was *your* life story. *Did I Shave My Ass For This?* was a huge hit. There is even talk of a film version. The judges just can't stand your astonishing sexiness! They didn't want you to win because you seem to have so much already."

"Yeah," Cliff said, encouraged. "Yeah. They are jealous! That must be it." He straightened up, boobs out.

"That's my guy!" David said.

They noted Becky Ridgeworth was out for a speed walk ahead. The speed walking seemed to be doing her good. She had lost quite a bit of weight, though Becky would never be model thin. She referred to herself as "volumptuous," and it looked good on her. She waved at David and Cliff gleefully. Still, her color was pale this day, and she seemed a bit lacking in her usual oomph.

The guys waved. "Hey there, Becks," David greeted as they met in the middle of the street in front of the Jones's old place. "You're walking alone. Where's Melinda today?"

"She's up with Cassie whining about something," Becky said. "Happy anniversary, guys!" She gave them each a kiss on the cheek.

"Thanks, sweetie," David said.

"Are you doing okay, Becks?" Cliff asked. "You look a bit under the weather."

"I think I may be coming down with something. Maybe a cold due to the change in season." She snorted. "And just in time for the Halloween party too. Ain't them the breaks?"

She leaned in closer to speak with more discretion, gathering Cliff and David to her so that she stood between the golf cart and the strong man. "Have you two met the newbies in the neighborhood?" she asked. "The ones who bought Steve and Sandy's place?"

"Not yet," said David, copying her lowered voice and cautious mannerisms. "We've yet to even see them, and they've been here a whole week."

"Well, I wouldn't be expecting them to come and introduce themselves. Especially not to you two. They're worse than Nanna Hench was, if you get my meaning. They're biblical literalists."

The three sinners slowly turned and stared at the Jones house. There was movement behind the curtain in the large living room window.

"Literalists?" David said.

"That's what Cassie says."

"What the hell are they doing on Jasper Lane?" David asked.

"Well," Becky said, "I can only guess, but we do have a nice temperate clime here. That's good stoning weather."

"They smoke weed?" Cliff asked.

David reached over and patted his hubby on the bicep. "Excuse him," he said to Becky. "He's been juicing something crazy of late." Then, back to Cliff: "No, sweetie. Stoning. With stones. Giving people ouchies."

They stared at the house silently, as if expecting it to defend itself from some of their accusations. Or at least expecting its residents to come out and offer some sort of denial. Then, as if from a horror film

8

with cheap special effects—like Syfy on a Saturday night—a family of four appeared in the window.

"Great Grant Wood!" David exclaimed. "*American Gothic* in duplicate!"

"They do look rather... plain," Becky said.

"How did they just appear like that?" Cliff asked.

"They're magic," Becky said in a hush. "Magic Christians."

Cliff grimaced. "Should we burn them?"

"They look angry," David noted.

It was then that the motherly-looking figure—if she could be called that—suddenly pointed at them and mouthed something indecipherable. The others in the family smiled with what looked like pride. Well, at least two of the others. The younger woman stood as stoic and expressionless as stone.

"What did that old bitch say to us?" David asked. "Can anyone read lips?"

"Heathen?" Becky gave it a try. "Heather? Heathcliff? Why would she call us Heathcliffs? Was that a fat joke? Like that cartoon cat?"

"I thought that was Garfield," Cliff said.

Becky turned to Cliff as if now completely involved in discussing cartoon felines. "Well, there was Garfield. But Heathcliff was another cat, and he had this big bruiser of a friend who was a dog—"

"Well, whatever she called us," David said, "that's enough of that!" He then redirected the poisoned dart back at the older woman with his own finger.

The foursome—seemingly not expecting this—looked horrified and immediately disappeared from view.

"Magic Christians!" Cliff swooned.

"What church do they go to?" David asked.

"The Church of Satan," replied Becky.

"No," said David. "I know Satan. Even he would think they were weird. Let's be the cool kids and mosey on away from here. I'm getting the creeps."

As he was speaking, Becky braced herself against the golf cart with her hand on her stomach.

"Everything okay, Becks?" Cliff asked.

"Yeah. I just need to sit down."

David and Cliff helped her into the cart.

"It's nothing," she said, trying to ease the concern on her friends' faces. "Probably a little gas. Every pregnant woman gets gas. That's the only time women get gas. Ever."

"Maybe that magic Christian lady put a curse on you when she pointed at us," David joked. "You can name the baby Rosemary."

Becky's pregnancy had been the talk of Jasper Lane for a few weeks now. Everyone wanted to know who the father was, but Becky refused to tell even Melinda. She had promised to one day give away the secret, but until then she spoke openly about how she was rather enjoying the infamy.

She sat a moment longer, letting the pain subside.

"Should we get her to a doctor?" Cliff asked David.

"No," Becky said. "I'm fine." She stood. "Look. I'm fine now."

"Still," David said, "why don't you let me drive you home in my trusty cart here?"

Becky reseated herself. "If it will make you feel better."

"Looks like we're leaving just in time," Cliff said with a nod at the new neighbors' house. The creepy younger woman was back in the window, her wiry hair the remnants of a bad perm job.

"Move over," Cliff said. "I'm coming too."

"You'll break the cart!" David protested. "I just got it fixed."

"Shut up and drive," Cliff replied. "Quick! Before someone comes out the door and starts throwing stones at us!"

Becky squealed as David sped away.

THEY weren't a family. Not really. They did call each other "brother" and "sister," but only in that "my God is your God" kind of way. There wasn't one drop of blood between them.

At dinner they sat together in the sparsely decorated dining room—a simple table set from the local Big Lots and a plain wooden cross on the wall—and they prayed. The room was flooded with light from an undressed chandelier, which washed all the color away. The food was ordinary and unseasoned. They had had the very same dinner since they had moved in: brown beans, white bread, and humility.

Their dress was just as ordinary as everything else. There were no flourishes here. Not in this house. A true house of salvation did not need flourishes. This family would show everyone else on Jasper Lane the Way. Just the four of them—Mr. Scott, Sally, Michelle, and... and the other one whose name easily escaped people's minds. Oh, yes. Newt. Everyone was always forgetting Newt. Michelle was mute, but Newt was just Newt.

Mr. Scott led the prayer, his voice gathering his small flock before their small meal. "Lord," he said with a hint of a put-on Southern accent, "thank you for the great bounty we are about to receive. We know we don't deserve it. We know, too, that we deserve it perhaps more than some. Yes. We know that very well, Lord.

"We thank you, Lord, for this day of life you have seen fit to give us. A day we have tried to do your will. A day we have most probably squandered." Mr. Scott eyed Michelle and Newt.

"We thank you for the ability to see sin where others cannot, so blinded by their lust are they.

"We thank you for your permission to go forth and punish those who sin most egregiously against thou... thine... er, thee.

"We thank you for showing us to Sister Hench, a woman as close to you as we strive to be ourselves. As pure a soul as one can expect in this degenerate world. A woman without whose help and deep passion we might have never found this street full of sin."

11

He was spitting passion all over his beans and bread.

"This street will be cleansed by the end of the year, Lord. That is our promise to you. And it begins with that nasty movie actor. The big one, with all the obscene muscles who jogs past our new home practically nude."

Sally flushed at the mention of this man. They had just seen him that very day, looking in at them from the street. They had decided then and there he would be the first. They would climb the biggest mountain first.

"His muscles…," Sally had said to Michelle when they were alone that afternoon preparing the meal. "Oh, Lord! I say a prayer within a prayer to stop thinking of those muscles. They make me crave steak. But you wouldn't understand, would you? You're just a dumb mute girl."

"In your name, Lord," Mr. Scott continued in his prayer. "Amen."

The rest of the (speaking) congregation echoed his final word, and all four quietly ate of their meal, each with their own little worlds and personal conversations eating away at their minds.

"I WAS worried I might have overdressed," Melinda said as she stood beside Terrence in a long line outside of *Vera's*. "But everyone looks so nice!"

They were surrounded by handsome men, beautiful women, and dazzling drag queens. Melinda wore a form-fitting black number—neither too casual nor too formal—while Terrence was dressed in something of equal standing and questionable gender.

"Of course everyone is dressed nice here," Terrence replied. "What were you expecting? This is a gay bar, not JCPenneys."

"I've never been to a gay bar," she said conspiratorially.

"Really? I couldn't tell." His sarcasm was lost on her.

"It's true. I've never been to any nightclubs at all, actually."

"Well, Vera was delighted when I told her you were coming here tonight. I would expect to be made a big deal of."

Melinda smiled politely at the others in the line. "Thank you for taking me out tonight, Terrence," she said. "I really needed this. To get out and go somewhere different."

"It's the least I could do after ruining your date with Mr. Lollipop—"

"Mr. Lintrope," she corrected him.

"Lintrope? What a ridiculous name. Honey, I did you a favor. You should buy me a drink tonight. I'll let you know when."

Melinda wasn't paying too much attention to what Terrence was saying. She was enthralled by what was happening around them. All the color. All the new slang. All the gesturing. My God! The gesturing!

"I'll tell you something else," Terrence continued. "One of those wrestlers who kindly and collectively gave me the breath of life had a little more oomph in his engine, if you know what I mean. He was definitely family."

"Terrence!"

"What? Calm down. They were all at least seventeen."

"Not that." Melinda tugged his sleeve. "I think that woman over there just winked at me."

Terrence turned to see. "Wink back. Get yourself a free drink out of it."

"Really?"

"Why not?"

She giggled. "I feel like a teenager at my first party."

They had reached the door, but the rope was pulled. A giant man at least a story high blocked their way. "Sorry," he said, clearly not at all sincere. "That's it for right now." He then waved a couple of younger men into the club.

"Terrence," Melinda said, "why isn't this frightening man letting us inside?"

"I don't know," Terrence answered. "Frightening man, why aren't you letting us in? We demand to be let in!"

"There's a limit," the man grumbled.

"I've seen this place packed to the strobe lights. If there's a limit, I've not been in it."

"An *age* limit."

Terrence was not happy. *"Do you know who I am?"*

The frightening man ushered another couple of young sluts inside. He even gave one of them a wink.

"Let's just go," Melinda said, hushed and embarrassed.

"We will not go!" Terrence screamed. "We will stay right here until Beefy Bottom Slut Bucket lets us in."

Vera's voice sailed over them before the bouncer had a chance to do to Terrence what his position called for. "What is all this ruckus?"

She came out dressed in red with her hair twirled up on the top of her head in a design that clearly had taken her wigmaker years.

"Melinda!" she said, indeed delightedly. "Why are you out here? Come inside this minute. Rufus, these are my friends. I told you to let them in."

"Sorry, ma'am," the bouncer said. "He looked younger in the photo."

Vera took both Terrence and Melinda by the hand and led them in through the crowd. Terrence turned and stuck out his tongue at the bouncer. The bouncer licked his lips at Terrence.

"Whore!" Terrence gasped.

Melinda was awed by the club. The lights and the ambience were brand-new to her. Everyone's heart here beat to the loud pulse of the music. She couldn't keep from showing her amazement at each new detail, at the crowded dark and the smell of sweat. Of sex. Her mouth was wide open as she looked this way and that. She was getting appreciative glances from women and even a few from some of the men. Bisexuals, she guessed.

"Now, you stay close to us," Terrence said as they split the crowd. "I don't want you to get lost on your first time here. I know it looks intimidating, but…."

"There are so many handsome men." Melinda marveled at the men in dance cages, dancing with each other. "And so much glitter!"

"Only the best at *Vera's*," said the club's proud owner. "Everything shines. Everything glitters."

The dance floor was filled with sweaty figures. Men gyrating on men. Women grinding on women. Drag queens doing strange things with feathered boas. And black was the signature style color.

Melinda could contain herself no longer. Before Terrence knew it, she had broken free of his grasp and sprinted off to the dance floor, where she soon found more than one dance partner of every sex and gender.

"What is she doing?" Terrence said. "She'll be eaten alive!"

"She's dancing," responded Vera in shock. "And she's… very good."

It was true. The dance floor loved Melinda Gold like the camera loved Tom Hardy. It was as if she had been dancing all her life. She was a star on the floor. Solid gold! The gays loved her.

Terrence and Vera found a table and waited for Melinda to come find them. Vera had drinks brought to the table. She was a regal queen watching over her nighttime wonderland. While they waited, Terrence summoned a posse of drag queens and told them of his cheerleading idea for James's rugby team. They ate it up, and every one of them wanted to be involved. One of them even had costumes—skirts, pom-poms, and all—from a dead drag show she had done a few years previous.

After fifteen minutes of boogying down with strangers, Melinda found Terrence and Vera again. "This is so much fun!" she said. "And look who I found."

Behind her were the resident lesbian Wiccans of Jasper Lane, Keiko and Asha. They hated being known as "the lesbian Wiccans," but they knew there was no way around it. Some people were just born to stand out.

"Hey there, ladies," Vera said.

"What did you all put in Melinda's drink to get her to come out this evening?" Asha asked.

"And dance!" Keiko said. "Girl, you can dance!"

Melinda smiled and shrugged. She pulled on Terrence's hand. "Come on, Terrence," she said. "Let's boogie."

"Moi?" he said. "Why, I'd love to!"

He rose and turned back to the queens who sat around Vera like extravagant courtiers. "Tomorrow, girls. Cheerleading tryouts begin."

Terrence, Melinda, Asha, and Keiko were soon swallowed up by the dance floor crowd.

"*That's* the infamous Melinda Gold?" one of the drag queens asked Vera.

"Mmmm-hmmmm," Vera said. "Terrifying, ain't she?"

"EXCUSE me," said the burly man as he stood in the open garage doorway. He was dressed in a brown delivery uniform that threatened to cut off circulation to his thick arms and legs. His face had a nicely trimmed dark beard, and he wore a brown hat.

Cliff had been moving boxes in the garage. He was dressed in a tank top and tiny useless blue jean shorts. He realized this was not the weather for such attire (his nipples were deadly from the chill), but the shorts just made him feel so damn sexy. His ass ate them up.

"Can I help you?" Cliff said. "A bit late to be making deliveries, isn't it?" He looked the bearded man up and down. It was a familiar game. They were muscle men sizing each other up.

"I'm new," the man said. "I got lost a while back. I was wondering if you might be able to help me."

16

Cliff had seen this film before. He had *been* in this film before. And he loved it. "Sure. I can help." He didn't smile. He knew to keep it impersonal.

Cliff reached into the glove department of David's car and pulled out a road map. He walked to the tool table slowly, letting his mass do the talking, and spread the map over the table as he bent over and spread his legs. He looked over his shoulder and gave the deliveryman admittance.

"What's your name?" Cliff asked.

The deliveryman approached and stood just behind him. "Rock."

"Of course it is."

Cliff arched his ass slightly so that it was just past irresistible.

"Listen, man," said Rock, "I'm straight. I just want directions."

"Do you?" Cliff asked, loosening the jean cut-offs and letting them fall to the floor. Rock began breathing harder, looking angry.

Cliff backed his ass into the bulge in Rock's pants, then moved his prized possession up and down the deliveryman's package.

"I want that," Cliff said. "I want that in me."

"I told you," said Rock, "I'm straight."

"That's not what your cock is saying. Shove it inside me, bitch."

That tipped it. It made the deliveryman furious. In a frenzy, he began unbuttoning his pants. "You want this?" he said as his cock fell out and hit Cliff's ass with a smack. "Fine. I'll give it to you, you filthy whore. I'm gonna tear your goddamn ass apart."

Rock grabbed Cliff's shoulders with one hand and played around with Cliff's hole with the other, pretending more than once as if he was going to relentlessly drive his dick inside, head to balls, only to let it slide between Cliff's cheeks. Once he went as far as to get the tip of the head in the hole before ducking out. The teasing was driving Cliff crazy.

"Fuck me," Cliff said. "Just fuck me!"

Finally, Rock pried Cliff open and slowly sank inside him. Cliff's knees buckled from the force. He let out a cry as Rock—a straight man, no less—pounded his man-pussy like he was a pro in the League of Man-Pussy Pounders. If Rock had a porn name, it would have been Jack Hammer. Cliff could hardly see straight.

"Take it!" Rock said. "Take it all! Your hot man ass will never again tempt an innocent straight man."

"Yeah. Teach me a lesson!"

"I'm taking one for the team!"

"Me too!"

Rock grabbed the two globes of Cliff's ass and pulled them apart. He stuck his thumbs into the edges of Cliff's hole so he could get his dick farther in, and he rutted like a beast, roaring and drooling as he went.

"What the hell is going on in here?"

There was a pause in the fucking. Everything was still. David stood at the garage door.

"Honey," Cliff said, breathless and sweaty and unable to move from being so heavily penetrated, "I can explain."

"I don't want to hear it!" David yelled. He reached over and shut the garage door. "But I *am* going to teach you a lesson."

He walked toward Cliff and Rock, undoing his own pants.

"Honey, no!" cried Cliff. "Not the... *doublefuck*! I'll never survive!"

"Shut up, bitch!" David said.

He crawled atop the table so that he straddled Cliff. His own ass was a well-toned piece of art.

"Make room for me, deliveryman," he said. "I'm coming in! Stretch him out."

"My poor beautiful ass!" Cliff yelled as he was pounded by both men, his asshole being stretched beyond all recognition. *Oh, the humanity!*

The garage was nearly shaken to the ground by all the commotion happening inside of it. The hollering and savage cursing, the cries of mercy and of *more!* were punctuated at last by a great caterwaul that caused neighbors to look out their windows and lock their doors. Afterward, Cliff, David, and the deliveryman lay in a heap on the garage floor. There would be quite a clean-up.

Cliff wrapped his arms around David. "Thank you, baby," he said.

"Happy anniversary," said David, and he gave Cliff a kiss.

Just then came an obtrusive knock. David rose, pulled on his pants, and hit the button to the garage door. A man dressed in similar fashion as Rock but without the beard stood with a lascivious grin.

"I seem to have lost my way," this new deliveryman said.

David looked at Cliff, who was grinning.

"You got me one too?" David said. "Aw, baby! You shouldn't have."

"Happy anniversary," Cliff said. "Now, the two of you get in here. Let's have some fun."

The Chapter in Which Cliff Gets a Flurby

MORNING on Jasper Lane, and holding court at the cul-de-sac were the Four Ladies—Cassie, Vera, Melinda, and Becky. Of course, they often invited others up for their morning ritual of gossip and jibing. Their morning coffees were not exclusive by any means. Sandy Jones had come on occasion when she still lived on Jasper Lane, as had Asha and Keiko. Even The Boys—Rick, Terrence (especially Terrence), James, David, and Cliff—occasionally made a showing. But this morning it was just the four of them, drinking what they thought appropriate breakfast beverages and nibbling on polite breakfast foods, all laid out on the patio table on beautiful porcelain dishes.

The sun was pleasant this morning. Some days it got too intense for them. They would need to put up a tarp. But that was in the summer, and it was well into fall now. The weather was more apt to offer a good soak than sunburn. And when it rained, refusing to have their tradition pissed on, the ladies would sit in Cassie's spacious living room. However, Cassie would always sigh and say of the situation, "It's just not the same." They would all agree with her assessment.

This morning Vera, Melinda, and Becky each wore stylish sunglasses and a floppy hat. This was not done on purpose or for any particular reason. This was not the beginning of a club outfit. They did not inquire via phone what each would be wearing. That would be silly. Individually it just felt like a floppy hat and sunglasses type day. Only two types of people can get away with wearing both a hat and sunglasses simultaneously, and they are country singers and extravagant ladies. This is something everyone knows.

Cassie was unique among the foursome in her attire. Yes. She wore sunglasses, but instead of a floppy hat, of which she had many, she wore a red-and-white silk scarf tied over her hair.

The ladies watched over the seasonably decorated neighborhood as they relaxed into slouches—even Melinda—in the ultra-comfortable new lounge furniture Cassie had purchased at a reduced price from some large store's going-out-of-business sale.

"It's a shame Sandy and Steve moved," Becky said, then sipped at her decaf and looked in the direction of the Jones's old home. "I miss her. She was a hoot. It will be good to see her tonight."

"Sandy is in town?" Vera asked.

"Just for tonight to finish up some things."

"It was a rather sudden move, wasn't it?" Cassie replied. "But I understand money was tight. And they had a couple of more… personal matters to see to."

"I'll tell you why they moved," Vera said. "To get away from us." She smiled. "We were just too much for them. They could not keep up."

"Sandy's departure definitely sent the Gay Porn Wives Club into a tizzy." Cassie adjusted her sunglasses. "What a ridiculous organization, anyway. Who thinks up things like that? I mean, really. And why didn't they ask me to be an honorary member?"

"Now who's going to host the annual Jasper Lane Fourth of July party?" Becky wondered. "They held it every year. I suppose we should decide that before too long."

Melinda sat straight up. "Me! I can do it. Oh, please let it be me!"

Without looking at her, Cassie reached over and gave her a gentle tap on the wrist. "Tag. You're it. I have enough on my plate with my porn parties and the Halloween bash every year. I'm thinking this street may be entirely too festive."

Melinda rested back into her chair, a broad smile on her face.

"Does anyone here know anything about this family that moved into Steve and Sandy's place?" Cassie wondered. "That is, anything we haven't yet discovered."

Becky and Melinda looked at one another and then leaned forward. "Haven't *yet* discovered?" Becky asked. "What *have* you discovered about them? We know next to nothing."

"Well,"—Cassie leaned toward them—"Vera and I did a little investigating the night they moved in, just to see how things were going and who the hell these people are. We don't want to be on the same street as a serial killer, do we?"

"Heavens, no," Melinda said.

"We hid in the bushes—"

"Dressed in black," Vera interrupted. "We were cat women and sexy as all hell. M-hmmm."

"We noticed that before they had a thing moved into the house, they were going around chanting and praying in every room."

"Damn strange shit!" Vera noted. Her golden bracelets jangled as she marked her exclamation.

"It was like they were trying to expel some bad spirits—"

"Or invite them in!"

Melinda sat back again slowly in her chair. "So they are fanatics… like my mother. A whole family of Nannas!"

"That's the thing," Cassie said. "I don't think they *are* a family. At least, not a biological family. When you get a good look at them, none of them even remotely resemble each other."

"And the young lady!" Vera said. "Tell them about *her*!"

"If she's one of their children then I'm Glenn Close!" Cassie said. "She's got the eyes of a thirty-year-old. She and the boy caught us spying on them. We tried to be all nice and play it off innocently as if we were lost and drunk, but that little bitch just gave us the look of death. Not a word either."

"The boy spoke, though," Vera said.

"Newt, I think he said his name was. He told us all of their names. I don't think he's playing with a full deck. We asked him where he was from and all he said was 'I just do what they tell me to do.' Then the older woman—Sally—came out of the house, saw us in the bushes, and freaked out."

"We headed back here, sprint-like."

Melinda, having recently discovered classic horror films and being quite intrigued by them, exclaimed, "Do you think they're... *Stepford children*?"

Vera took hold of her hand. "Honey," she said with a condescending edge and a shake of the head.

"Perhaps we should get our resident law woman, Asha, on the case," Cassie said. "Just to get a little background check on our new friends."

"Is that legal?" Melinda asked.

Cassie shrugged. "How the hell do I know?" She took a drink of her alcoholic coffee beverage, then looked at Melinda with a smile. "Are you still angry with Terrence about yesterday?"

Melinda sighed. "No. Not really. I'm still a *bit* irritated, but I think that maybe it was for the best."

"The librarian was no Coach Nipple, huh?"

"What? No. That's not it all. It's just.... Yes. I suppose that is it."

"You want your Nipple back, honey?" Vera grinned.

Melinda gave her a swat. "Stop it."

"I can guarantee you that Mr. Lintrope would never have taken you dancing," Vera said. "And, my lady, you can dance."

"I really can!" Melinda said. "And I'm as surprised as you. Who knew I had those genes."

Becky began to laugh, but her glee was cut short by a sharp pain.

"Becky," Cassie said, "I've noticed you've been holding your side all morning. Is everything okay?"

"I'm peachy," she said. "Just peachy."

There was a silence between the foursome. Glances bounced from one set of eyes to another over who would be the one to dig deeper and open up Becky's fib. Something was on the verge of being said by Cassie when Becky suddenly pointed to the street and chirped, "What do you suppose she's doing?"

Down below on Jasper Lane, standing on the street in front of the Jones's old place, was the young woman, the mute named Michelle. She was facing the cul-de-sac. Cassie reached for her binoculars and peered down the street. The girl was looking right at them, dressed in a loosely-fitted gray flowered gown that even Dull would call "dull." Her hair was a mess of red that was twisted by the breeze.

"I can't see her eyes too well," Cassie said, "but I can report that is one crazy-looking young woman."

"What do you think she's doing?" Melinda asked.

"At the moment," Vera said, "becoming a speed bump if she doesn't move out of the street." She rose and yelled down, "Move, you crazy bitch!"

DAVID awoke as Cliff came into the bedroom with an affectionate "Good morning, baby." He had made breakfast again. David sat up, wiped the sleep from his eyes, and smiled. They'd had quite a night. The tricks had left early in the morning.

"You're spoiling me," he said in a soft voice. "My next husband will never be able to compete."

Cliff set the tray over David's legs and then sat down next to him. He was showered and dressed in sweats and a tank top. Cliff had been up for a couple of hours already so he could get a bit of morning cardio in before making breakfast for the two of them. Because of his hard training, the breakfasts Cliff made were spectacular. Eggs, waffles, thick strips of bacon, toast, sausage, and juice. And he wasn't even bulking anymore.

"You know," David reminded his hubby, "I'm not in training like you are. This will all turn to fat on me. My muscles aren't as hungry as yours."

Still, he picked up one of the pieces of toast Cliff had lovingly cookie-cut into hearts (a tradition) and he began to eat, dipping it into the syrup. He leaned over and gave Cliff a kiss on the cheek.

Cliff didn't touch the food. Instead he leaned back on the headboard, hands behind his head.

"What's wrong, babe?" David asked, his mouth full of toast.

"Maybe I made a mistake," said Cliff. "I've been thinking that maybe I should have stayed with porn. I can still get back into it. I'm a superstar there. You saw me last night."

"Why would you want to do that?"

"The usual. Because I'm nervous." He looked at David pleadingly. "What if I can't make this bodybuilding thing work? I mean, you should see the size of some of the guys who compete."

"You're just as big as they are."

"But there is a difference to our bigness. You might not be able to see it, but other bodybuilders can. It's all about perfect symmetry."

"Sounds like high school. Like cliques. Muscle cliques."

"You're not too far off. And everyone is always looking for that edge to make them the most popular."

"That's life in general." David faced Cliff. "You listen to me. You will always be Mr. Popular to me."

Cliff smiled and gave David a kiss. Such gentleness from such a large man. "I guess I'm just going through withdrawal. The daily adoration on set was intoxicating. I don't guess I'll ever feel that way again."

"Well, then," David said, putting the tray carefully on the floor, "it looks like I haven't been doing my job. Let me adore you."

He moved in closer, kissing Cliff on the lips, the chin, the neck, the chest, and then the underarms. Cliff flinched and giggled, bringing his huge arms down tight to his sides. David was not deterred. Upon reaching Cliff's bodybuilder belly, David lifted up the shirt and gave Cliff a loud flurby on the belly button. Cliff howled in laughter, trying to protect his ticklish tummy from David's wet, noisy lips. To no avail. Cliff would not escape. There would be tickling.

JUST down the street and out of the sheets, Rick Cooper-Tucker and his own piece of manliness, James, were rising to meet the day. One could have put a camera on the two and sold it as an ad to a gay greeting card company, so content was their morning interaction. In fact, Keiko, the street's resident filmmaker (and now, thanks to Cliff, even more famous for directing high-quality gay porn), had once filmed them for just that, though the footage was never used. Rick was sure it would surface one day when he was much older and had a much weaker heart.

Before leaving for his job at the fitness center, Rick started the computer in the kitchen. It was an older desktop they only used occasionally when they were cooking and needed to browse the Internet for recipes. As the computer loaded, Rick could hear James watching television in the den. Rick drummed his fingers along the kitchen table, fixed his eye patch, and checked his wristwatch while waiting for the old relic of a computer to wake up. Sometimes it acted up so badly both of them wondered why they kept it at all. When finally he was able to get into his e-mail, his shoulders slumped at the meager sight of only five messages, and two of them were spam that had somehow gone unfiltered. He clicked on a message from Terrence:

> *YOU WILL LOVE THIS. SHOW IT TO YOUR PORN-OBSESSED HUBBY ;-) Just kidding! Love ya both! (But he is a porn freak. You know that, right?)*
>
> *Loves!*
>
> *T*

Rick grinned and clicked on the link he had been sent. There was nothing wrong with a little perviness to start the day. It might shock him to full waking life. The page came up as "Forbidden." He gave the computer a confused look.

He tried again with the same response. Was the old thing finally dying?

He walked to the den and found James watching an episode of *Star Trek*—one of the myriad of spin-offs from the original futuristic program... with nary a single gay character in the lot.

"James," Rick said, "have you noticed something wrong with the kitchen computer? Terrence sent me a link, and when I tried to click on it, a message came back saying it was forbidden."

"Was it porn?" James asked, not taking his eyes off the television. He was slumped into the sofa, becoming one with it. Very Zen.

"Of course it was. It was a link from Terrence. What else would he send?"

"Well, there you have it. I installed parental controls. It blocks all the porn."

"Why would you do that?" Rick leaned onto the back of the sofa.

"I think I might be developing a problem with porn. I've been looking at way too much of it lately. I'm addicted to the nasties. I want to nip this problem in the butt."

"Bud."

"Huh?"

"Bud. You want to nip it in the bud."

"I don't think so. I'm sure it's butt."

"It's not, but your perseverance is admirable. What will you do all day with no porn to look at?"

James shrugged. "I was thinking of trying to find a job."

"Doing what?"

"I don't know. Something besides living off my uncle's inheritance. I have some great training from the army. That's good for something."

Rick massaged James's shoulders. "What about that superhero comic book you were working on? That kept you busy for a while. What was it called?"

"*The Adventures of Big Wiener & Little Bunghole.*"

Rick snickered. "Yeah. What about that?"

"It petered out."

"Clever."

James pointed the remote at the television program in gesture. "Sometimes I feel like Commander Riker. Like I'm the Commander Riker of Jasper Lane."

"Powerful? Bearlike?"

"No. Boring. Compared to the other characters on the show, so fucking boring."

"You are far from boring." Rick bent and kissed James on the top of the head. "Stop all this talk. I'm going to work. You should come with me. Maybe you'll get an idea of what you want to do with your days while you work out."

"I'll be there later. I'm going to sit here with my hand down my pants a bit longer. Maybe contemplate my white breadness on a street of gooey cinnamon rolls."

Rick gave James's shoulders a final squeeze before leaving. "Take the parental controls off the computer, darling. You may have sworn off porn, but I haven't."

"Fine," James said. "Feed my addiction."

CASSIE BLOOM and Becky Ridgeworth tossed bags of Halloween candies into the shopping cart indiscriminately. Cassie grabbed at bags on the left and Becky snagged bags on the right as they pushed the cart along, directly centered in the aisle. The cart's contents were a colorful array of candy corns, ghostly marshmallows, and chocolate-covered ghouls. When some rude shopper wanted past them, there were shows of dazzling annoyance from Cassie. This encouraged said shopper to hurry on by to avoid being stared at quite so strongly.

They had changed from their morning attire and were now dressed in autumn browns and twills. Cassie's hair had been lightened by the summer sun, and she wore her large sunglasses perched on her head as she surveyed the candy land. Becky wore her hair in a ponytail that bounced as she bobbed along to the song playing on the store's sound system. Becky was able to take off work in the middle of the day and go candy shopping with Cassie because she now made her own hours at the production company. She did not have an ordinary job. But then, no one had an ordinary job. At least, no one on Jasper Lane.

"What is this?" she asked, bobbing and swaying. "What song is this?"

Cassie stopped to listen. "I have no idea," she said after a moment. "Something sweet and lovely to keep us in the store. It's manipulation. Everything is manipulation these days."

Cassie picked up a bag of pumpkin-shaped peanut butter cups. She tore it open, and she and Becky each took one before she put the bag in the cart with the rest of the candy.

"So what's going on with your stomach?" Cassie asked. She gave Becky an arched eyebrow. "You're going to have to tell me at some point. Best be when Melinda and Vera aren't around."

"It's—"

"It's not *nothing*. Nothing's ever *nothing*. And it looks even less like nothing the longer you wait."

Becky bit into the peanut butter cup. "I don't know. At first I was thinking it was just normal pregnancy stuff. But sometimes… the pain…."

Cassie stopped and faced her. "Promise me you will see a doctor again. And don't wait three weeks until your next appointment."

"Do you think it might be that serious? That much of 'not *nothing*'? I don't want to be one of these women who turn into reactionaries when they get preggers."

"Darling," Cassie said as they resumed their stroll down the aisle, "all women become reactionaries when they get pregnant. It's unavoidable. It's completely natural. Promise me you'll join the club."

"I'll go see a doctor. I promise." She sighed. "I should have seen problems like this coming along from conception."

"What do you mean?"

"Do you remember I told you that the father is one of the actors at the studio in the bisexual genre? How we got a bit drunk at a party last summer and he left a bit of himself behind?"

Cassie gave Becky a wicked grin. "I do. You mean there's more to tell?"

Becky took an aggressive bite from another peanut butter cup. "While we were going at it, another of the guys in the line stumbled into the room. When I say 'stumbled', I mean it. He was trashed. I believe he thought we were filming a scene in a new movie and…."

Cassie's mouth dropped open. "He didn't!"

"Yep. He came up behind my guy and stuck it right into him. He didn't even lube first. You should have heard the holler."

"It didn't go over too well, huh?"

"Better than you'd think. After the initial shock, we all kind of got into it." She looked guiltily at Cassie. "It was hot."

Cassie fanned herself. "Oh dear."

"I used to get so irritated with Sandy when she was pregnant with Amy. She would worry so much that she was going to be a horrible mother. That she hadn't the qualifications. But I get it now."

"Just because your baby has kinda/sorta two daddies does not mean you're going to be a bad mother. My son, Jason, had one very real father, and I'll take either of the ones that were piled on top of you over him any day."

"Have you heard from Jason recently?"

"Not for weeks. Not for goddamn weeks."

"I'm sorry, Cassie."

Cassie gave her an appreciative smile. "Come on. Let's get out of this aisle before we have to be lifted by crane."

FROM the sidewalk, Melinda watched with amusement and crossed arms the spectacle happening in Terrence's front yard. Terrence was dancing around with a group of six other grown men in *girls'* cheerleading uniforms: bright orange miniskirts and matching sweaters with "Mean Girls" scrawled across their amplified chests. They each shook pom-poms, and a few of them even wore wigs and makeup. Terrence, of course, led the group in blonde pigtails and held the megaphone while barking out exhausted, often shrill commands. There were drinks aplenty, and there was a large trampoline that was getting quite a bit of attention from everyone involved. Still, whatever it was Terrence was doing, it was clear that nothing was truly getting done. Too much fun was being had.

From what Melinda could hear, Terrence and the Mean Girls were arguing over what song to listen to as they trained. There was a fierce debate over this matter, layered with colorful metaphors. An old boom box sat on a stool beside the trampoline. Dance tracks played continuously. Terrence stood protectively in front of the boom box and argued with four of his cheerleaders. The two others seemed oblivious, practicing splits in the air on the trampoline.

"Lucretia! Liza!" Terrence screamed at the jumping cheerleaders. "Get down from there! We're discussing terribly important matters, you sluts."

But a new track came over the boom box and Terrence lit up, laying his fury aside. "Oh my God! *It's Kylie!*"

They all screamed like teenage girls and aligned in a triangle on the grass in front of the trampoline, where they began dancing a choreographed jig to the pop star's megahit. Melinda laughed at the sight.

"I've created a monster," James said as he approached Melinda from behind, dressed in his gym wear.

"*You* did this?" Melinda asked.

"I helped. I told him he should put together a cheerleading squad for my rugby team. Terrence is always looking for something to do, isn't he? He's made 'personality in crisis' a career."

"Oh, James. Poor you."

"Poor us. We're *all* going to have to listen to this… training."

Neither of them noticed Mr. Scott until he had crept up beside them. He was dressed in a blindingly white suit. So white it left a blur stream.

"Disgusting!" the old man said. "Perverse."

Melinda and James looked at one another. "I don't know," Melinda said. "I think they're just having a little fun. You're name is Mr. Scott, right?"

Mr. Scott leered at her, shaking a finger. "You should know better. *You* were raised better!"

"Excuse me? Have we met?"

He walked away without an explanation, toward his own yard, where there was yet another spectacle in occurrence. His family had dragged onto their lawn a massive, thick wooden cross as white as Mr. Scott's suit. The young boy, Newt, was in the midst of digging a hole for the cross to be sunk into as Mr. Scott watched approvingly.

The Mean Girls all stopped their frivolity and watched the raising of the cross. The mood on Jasper Lane had changed tremendously. The temperature even seemed to dip. Like cold Hell.

"Well, *they* look like a blast," James said, nodding to the strange new family.

Melinda saw Terrence fumbling angrily with the boom box, taking out one cassette before putting in another. Very soon the recognizable opening chords of Madonna's "Like a Prayer" hummed predictably through the neighborhood. Of course, it was a dance version and had already been choreographed by the squad. Madonna was a prerequisite to membership in the Mean Girls. They dedicated the dance number to the new family as the cross made its ascent.

"Oh, for heaven's sake," Melinda said.

JAMES watched as Cliff threw around some serious weight at Hot Body Gym. Everyone in the fitness center was dumbfounded by Cliff's feats of strength, and he never failed to attract an audience whenever he trained. He didn't seem to mind the eyes. In fact, he encouraged them with the occasional flexing routine thrown in. Flexing routines made it acceptable for a straight man to feel another man up without being labeled as "gay." Only "impressed."

James looked at the massive dumbbells Cliff was curling. Then he looked down to his own.

"Are you fucking kidding me?" he mumbled.

He had once told Rick that sometimes Cliff turned him on in the weight room. This made Rick laugh, but it irritated James.

"Damn! I need to look at some porn!" James whispered.

Most people in the gym tried to see to their own workouts in between gawking at Cliff, but there were always a few who were so obvious that even James looked at them with annoyance. Michelle and Sally—the ladies from the new "family" on Jasper Lane—seemed to be taking an abnormal amount of interest in Cliff. They hadn't done a thing since they had come into the fitness center soon after James. They stood only a bit off from Cliff and watched him work out. The older one—Sally?—was open-jawed and blushing violent red as she watched, but the younger one, Michelle, stared at Cliff with an intense vacancy. She had deep, dark eyes, and her stringy red hair made her seem as mad as a hatter.

There, too, among the dumbbells was Coby. Coby was Rick's ex. He had been the one responsible for the loss of his eye. Coby, wearing sunglasses *inside* the fitness center, leaned on a weight rack and watched Cliff with what was either lust or jealousy. When he caught James looking in his direction, he quickly ducked out of the fitness center altogether. James watched him until he was out the door.

Then, in this parade of personal annoyances, he spotted Seth.

Seth. James's onetime friend and teammate, now turned rage-inducing scum who had tried to steal Rick right out from under him. If James felt a pinch of jealousy when he saw Coby, he was sacked in the stomach by it whenever he saw Seth. And Seth never learned. Even after getting his ass whipped—no, *whooped!*—by James, he still flirted with Rick, at times quite obviously. As James watched him now, Seth's gaze followed Rick around the fitness center as Rick picked up loose weights and cleaned off machines. Whenever Rick bent over, Seth's face got an expression like a dog in heat. A big ugly dog with missing teeth. In heat.

James kept his eyes locked on Seth. Rick finally migrated to somewhere in the fitness center behind James, and Seth caught James staring him down. The toothless dog held up a hand in sign of retreat and turned his attention to his workout. James, his body clearly boiling in testosterone, relaxed. There would be no physical altercation this day.

"Baby," Rick said, standing behind James. How long he had been there James did not know. "Staring down romantic rivals who don't exist doesn't make for a good hobby."

James turned to face him. "I want to beat him up. Can I beat him up?"

"No. Pump some iron. Then go to the store. We need milk."

James half smiled. "I can do that. But I really want to beat him up."

THE trip to the mailbox was both ever the highlight and the low point of Cassie Bloom's day. There was always hope that waiting for her inside the elegant little black mailbox would be a postcard or—dare to dream—even a letter from her son, Jason. Aside from two postcards, however—neither of which offered any clue as to where he was—she had not heard from him since he had disappeared earlier in the summer. He had simply written on the first (a picture of hills and mountains), *I'm fine. Don't worry.* And on the second (a worrying photo of a Jesus statue framed by trees), *Still fine.*

"Well," she had said with a shrug when the second one arrived, "at least our communication has improved."

She was worried sick, though. So worried that she couldn't even enjoy her tasty libations on some nights. She had tried calling him, of course, but his cell phone was no longer in use. It was quite irritating. She needed to have a tracking device implanted into her troubled son's thick head.

Hope. Every time she made a trip to the mailbox. Her heart pounding with excitement even before the mailman turned onto Jasper Lane. Her heart nearly bursting when she heard the clang of the box, thinking that maybe—just maybe—something from Jason was waiting for her. And then her heart breaking yet again when she read every name but his on the return addresses.

This day was no different. There was nothing from Jason, and her heart sank. But there was a large brown package from Melinda's son, Patrick Gold. This gave Cassie some delight. They had become friends, she and Patrick. She adored him. She didn't wait to get back inside the house before opening it. Inside there was a DVD with a yellow adhesive note attached.

"*For your next porn party*," Cassie read aloud.

She tore the adhesive from the front cover of the DVD and saw Patrick's college-boy face smiling back at her. He stood alongside other young men of equally charming demeanors, all of them nearly naked. Some were quite a bit more muscular than Patrick. Cassie knew immediately what kind of video this was. Patrick had let some jackass talk him into being in one of those spring break *All-American Guys Get All Nasty* videos, this one titled *Bros Bare All*.

Cassie sighed and turned to look down the street at Melinda's house.

"Oh, Patrick," Cassie said with a smile. "What will your mother say?"

MELINDA was surprised to see Cassie at her door.

"Can we talk?" Cassie said. "It's about Patrick."

"Sure. Come in."

Melinda led Cassie to the kitchen. She found that she liked chatting in the kitchen more than the living room. The living room— once her pride and joy—now seemed so stuffy. It reminded her of Nanna. She meant to get it redecorated as soon as she had the time… and money. She hated to admit that part, but everybody was hurting. Even the cosmetics industry.

"Is everything okay?" Melinda asked, getting a mug for Cassie and then pouring coffee for them both.

"Everything is fine," Cassie answered. "It's just—and don't get upset. Remember he's a college boy. It's just—"

The phone rang. Melinda sensed that whatever Cassie was about to tell her was not good, but she *had* to answer the phone. Melinda could never just let a phone ring. Crazy people did that. Poor people avoiding bill collectors did that. Melinda Gold did not do that.

Melinda held up a finger in gesture of "one minute" and answered the call.

"Melinda," the droll voice on the other end said, "it's Bethany."

Melinda's sister Bethany was searching for information on their real mother, their real family. The family Melinda and Bethany had been taken from when they were babies. Bethany was doing most of the detective work, and she called occasionally to let her sister know how things were progressing, if at all.

"Have you found out anything new?" Melinda asked in a lower and more cautious voice.

Cassie took her coffee and cast her glances elsewhere while Melinda talked with Bethany.

"Not yet," Bethany replied. "That's why I'm calling. You need to go talk to Nanna and get some information for me."

"Me? Why me?"

"Because one of us has to, and you're closer."

"I don't think proximity should really matter. Not when you're talking about Nanna. In fact, I think distance would be ideal."

"Melinda, I'm in Alabama. I've got a lead I'm chasing here. You can do this. Don't take any of her guff. Remember, she's not really your mother. She's nothing to us at all."

Melinda heard a brilliant and sharp edge to her sister's voice.

"Well… what should I ask her?" Melinda inquired.

"Start with the most obvious. Ask her who our mother is and ask her where we can find her."

"She won't tell us. She doesn't even know we know."

"Well, then tell her. Then threaten her."

"Bethany, I can't threaten. I can barely raise my voice."

"Bullshit."

"Bethany!" Melinda gasped.

"Do you want to find our mother or not?"

"Of course—"

"Then you need to do this. I need you to do this. Patrick needs you to do this. Don't forget how that old bitch treated him. And then, when it's done, when we've gotten everything we can from her, that old woman is going down. For good."

"Okay," Melinda said. She remembered how Nanna had berated Patrick. How she had smacked him on more than one occasion for

37

some silly reason. How Patrick was never good enough for the old woman. "Okay," she said again with more resolve.

After a few more words between them—their relationship had never been very deep—Melinda hung up and stood for a moment lost in her memories and regrets.

"Melinda?" Cassie said. "Maybe we should talk later? That sounded like a pretty serious conversation."

"Yes," Melinda said, distracted. "Yes. Later would probably be best, Cassie. Thank you."

"I'll see myself out, then."

Melinda stayed put in the kitchen as Cassie left. She wondered how she would approach this situation. She had done everything in her power to think as little as possible about Nanna. But now she had promised to once again stare the monster in the face. And that was a hideous face.

BECKY met her good friend (and former Jasper Lane resident) Sandy Jones for dinner at one of the trendy eateries that had popped up in town seemingly overnight. Sandy was back in town to tie up loose ends regarding the sale of the house. She had wanted to smooth things over with the Gay Porn Wives Club as well but soon realized that was a lost cause. Those bitches hated her now. She had nearly torn their cohesive whole asunder.

Sandy was dressed elegantly and hip, with a colorful silk scarf around her neck. She had cut her hair short and was pulling the look off quite well. Becky noticed she was quite fidgety, though. When she asked about this, Sandy beamed at her and said, "It's the energy pills. I'm taking them like candy. I'm getting so much done now that I'm on them. It's an addiction. I know that. But a healthy one."

"Sandy," Becky said over her pasta, "I don't think taking speed in pill form qualifies as healthy."

"Well, no. Maybe not for me. But it's worked wonders on mine and Steve's relationship. I don't sleep a lot, so we're together a lot more now."

She said it all with the smile of a Dentyne commercial.

"Jesus, Sandy! Please don't have a heart attack tonight. I don't know if I have the coping mechanisms for a coronary this evening."

Sandy laughed in a high-pitched, highly irregular manner and took a drink of wine. "How are things on the Lane?" she asked. "How's my little Cliff?"

"As big as life. That fella can pack on muscle faster than a clam. If there is ever an actual zombie apocalypse and I'm bitten, I'm going after him. His ass alone would keep me going for a week."

"I miss him. I need to come by and see him."

"You really do."

"But where's the time?" Sandy said. "If it's not one thing, it's another. I want to pull my hair out at times. That's why I cut it short."

"So, how is the little one? How is Amy?"

"Sweet and giggly. If I had her energy, I wouldn't need these pills." She reached across the table and grabbed Becky's hand. "And now you're going to be a mom too! Are you excited?"

"Yes," Becky said.

"I know that 'yes.' It's filled to the brim with worry. And I know from experience that there is nothing I can say to alleviate any of your doubt." She squeezed her friend's hand. "It's a lot of work. But it's also a lot of fun."

"And a lot of pills?"

"A few. Maybe. But I think you'll be able to cope with it better. You don't have a husband to get in your way." She squealed. "Oops. Did I say that? I can't believe I just said that."

"I imagine I'll have plenty of help from the Boys. David and Cliff are quite nurturing."

Sandy laughed convulsively again, scaring Becky just a little. "How is the new neighbor settling in? Have they called the cops on Terrence yet?"

"They're very odd, actually," Becky replied. "And the young woman is just plain scary."

"Young woman?" Sandy said, perplexed. "No. The house was sold to an older—and, might I add, very wealthy—person without any family. There was no young woman."

"Really?" Becky leaned forward, a net for more information. "Was this older person named Scott? Mr. Scott?"

"Maybe. We didn't have any real dealings with the actual buyer. It was all done through an agent. But the buyer was most definitely alone. I know that because the agent told Steve and me that whoever was buying the house was extremely antisocial and did not want to be bothered."

"Well, that's strange."

"Isn't it?" Sandy giggled. "They moved to the wrong neighborhood to not be bothered."

THAT night Jasper Lane was quiet and cool. A fall breeze was settling in. Most everyone was asleep or on their way to bed. But there were a few who used the darkness to keep watch over the neighborhood. Most notably the new "sin-turions" who lived at the Jones's.

Mr. Scott and Michelle stood to the side of David and Cliff's home, hidden behind some well-groomed shrubbery. They waited there for an hour, spying until the lights were turned off on the first floor and the only light left on in the house was that from the upstairs bedroom. They knew by now, after keeping close watch on all the neighbors for a week, that Cliff liked to step outside at night just before bed and have a snack. They watched him this night as he sat on the porch steps in boxers and a T-shirt and ate a muffin of some kind, most probably bran.

"Is everything set up for tomorrow?" Mr. Scott whispered to Michelle.

She said nothing. She only nodded.

"Good, my mute angel. It begins."

He smiled broadly. He would have even broken into a cackle if one thing had not jolted him out of his fanatic fantasy. They were not, as they had first assumed, the only souls up and waiting behind those bushes. Behind them came a low growl followed by a sharp bark. They turned and saw the neighborhood dog, an animal Mr. Scott had heard Melinda Gold call "Greyhound," or something to that effect. The animal looked at the two of them with contempt and started barking more ferociously.

Cliff stood up from the porch steps to see what the matter was, but by that time Mr. Scott had sprinted home, leaving Michelle standing there alone.

Cliff did not seem to see her, though if he had neared the bushes, he certainly would have. When he stepped toward her, she quickly vanished, leaving only Gayhound there, wagging his tail as Cliff approached. Cliff gave him a good pet on the head.

"What's wrong, boy?" he said, knowing that Gayhound often used the spot for his canine hookups. "Was there another critter in your love nest?"

Eric Arvin

The Chapter With Nanna and the Chair Lift

As EARLY as noon the next day, Terrence and his Mean Girls were once again in the front yard practicing their routines on the trampoline. The trampoline was, in fact, pointless to their future cheer spectacles. Such a thing would never be allowed on the sidelines of the pitch. But it made things more fun for the squad. The higher they bounced, the more athletic they felt.

Inspired by the chillier weather that day, they accessorized in pink leg warmers. This retro look, in turn, brought about the decision to cheer out to pure 1980s bubblegum pop. Harry, the man Terrence had met at the father/son outing with Christian, was the very first audience for the day. He sat in a lawn chair and Terrence gave him the task of controlling the boom box. He looked distinctly out of place in his plaid shirt and blue jeans, but he didn't seem to mind. Gayhound sat on the ground beside him and occasionally moaned at the goings-on.

No one truly seemed to notice Sally creeping over from the Jones's old place like a cautious mole. She was just as good as Mr. Scott in her creeping aptitude. But then, Terrence was making such a show of things with the queens that it was quite understandable for her to go unnoticed. It was only after she had come up from behind Harry and smashed the boom box beside him with a hammer that she registered any importance at all. Gayhound went into a fit of barknation. Terrence flew out of a triple spiral flip, jumped off the trampoline, and into a rage.

"You crazy bitch!" Terrence screamed. "That was vintage! Vintage! Just as old as you!"

"You're an abomination!" Sally screamed back. Then, with a broad hand gesture: "You're all abominations to the Lord!"

"And here I was thinking you were the sane one in your family," Terrence replied. "Missy, you take your hammer and your self-styled gray wig and go on home before I abominate *you*!"

Harry tried to calm Terrence down, putting a hand on his shoulder. Gayhound nipped at Sally, who kicked at him in return.

"No," Terrence said. "No! No! No! I am not having this bitch coming over here to my pretty house willy-nilly and messing with my pretty things." He lurched forward and grabbed the hammer from her. She jumped. "This is mine now!" Terrence hissed.

There was an audible gasp from Sally and many giggles from the Mean Girls.

"Repent!" Sally screamed.

By now, anyone who was home on Jasper Lane was watching the proceedings. Even Mr. Scott, Newt, and Michelle had come out of the house to support their fellow Christian warrior.

"You're a bad, mean woman," Terrence said. "You ain't nothing but a cliché! A stereotype. Is that what you want to be? A stereotype?"

Sally quickly surged forward again and knocked the remains of the boom box off the stool. Then she turned and ran toward her own house, screaming, "Repent! Repent!"

Terrence looked around at everyone, his mouth wide open and the hammer raised above his head as if he were keeping it out of Sally's reach. There was a pause where anyone could feel an explosion was imminent. Then Terrence screeched in glass-shattering volume, "*What the fuck was that?*"

BECKY feared she might have made a mistake.

The pangs in her belly had been intense that morning. So intense that, in a moment of desperation, she had called her father and told him what was going on. She regretted it almost immediately. Her father was a no-nonsense man who had been raised on and owned a pig farm. He believed in straightforward answers and, where Becky was concerned, he believed he was the only one who could offer her those answers. He was her life's encyclopedia.

"I'll be there as soon as I can," he told her in his husky voice over the phone. "Check yourself into a hospital."

"I don't need to do that, Daddy. And you don't need to come see me either."

"Becks, you do what your pappy tells you! I'm worried sick."

"What was that? Sorry, Daddy. You're breaking up. I can't hear you—"

"Becks, dammit! We're both on landlines."

Click.

"I have got to remember to get rid of my landline," she mumbled.

Now she would surely be getting a visit from her father, and very soon. She loved him, of course, but he had never forgiven her for growing out of her role as Daddy's Little Girl. He would try to implement old times and old roles upon arrival. Unlike Mr. Ridgeworth, Becky hadn't the fond memories of pig-farming life. She still remembered the name-calling and taunts from her classmates.

Thankfully her stomach had calmed since earlier when she had called him. But she was still worried. Maybe her pappy was right. Maybe she should check into a hospital, just for a night. Just until a few tests were taken and everything came back as perfectly fine. She *had* promised Cassie, after all.

"You're fine." She rubbed her belly. "You are fine and dandy. You're just sassy. That's all."

The doorbell rang and she answered, happy to have a distraction. Melinda was there, smiling, big and needy.

"Can I ask you a favor?" Melinda said. Her hands folded together in gesture of a prayer. It was not out of the question to think she had, in fact, prayed before coming over. Especially if she thought Becky might turn down her request.

"Would you like to come in first?"

"Thank you." Melinda stepped into the hall. "I'm sorry. I'm just so frazzled."

"Whatever is the matter, Mel?"

"Would you come with me to see Nanna?"

Becky was surprised. "Why would you want to see her again? I thought you had cut her out of your life completely."

"It's not a 'want' so much as it is a 'need'? She has some information, or at least my sister Bethany thinks she does, that might be helpful in our search for our real family."

"Why do you need me?"

"Not so much a 'need' as…."

"You want a buffer." Becky smiled. "Let me get my jacket." She opened the hall closet door to retrieve a coat. "You do mean now, right?"

"Yes! Yes. Thank you so much. I'll owe you a big basket of blueberry muffins for this."

"I'm not promising to keep my cool, though," Becky said as she put on the coat. "And I'll just warn you now, this may result in criminal charges."

"Bethany and I are waiting until after we've found our real family to press charges against her."

"You misunderstand. I meant charges by *her* against *me*."

COBY was such a skinny thing—all sticks and wires—that looking natural in the weight room would never happen. He stood in front of the dumbbell rack as his eyes darted from one size to another. He wasn't truly at Hot Body Gym to work out, but he didn't want Rick to see him standing around doing nothing. That could mean trouble. So he wore a torn T-shirt and crinkled shorts, both of which looked a size too large on him, and he sat on a bench to do some curls with the chosen set of dumbbells.

He thought he was doing pretty well too. Sure, he wasn't curling the extreme amounts the bigger guys did, but what he *was* doing hurt. And that was good. At least, he thought so. No pain, no gain.

His attention was on Rick as his former boyfriend straightened the racks around the fitness center. Coby's routine had become lopsided due to his wandering mind. He hadn't noticed that he had done a mere three repetitions on one arm and then fifteen on the other. It was at this point, on the fifteenth curl, that Rick finally noticed him. Coby nodded, trying to be sexy and cool, and then his arm gave out and he dropped the small weight on his toe. He jumped up with a screech.

Rick started toward him, but Coby smiled and waved off his help. "I'm fine," he said. More quietly, to himself, he whispered, "Ouch! My pride."

The embarrassment of having his toe smashed by his own apparent lack of strength and dexterity in front of Rick had distracted Coby from his purpose. That purpose being Cliff. The big guy had finished his training for the day and hit the showers. Coby slyly tried to follow him, a limping *Trainspotting* refugee.

Cliff was already showering when Coby made it into the locker room. He tried to blend into the scenery as he watched the muscle man lathering up the creeks and crevasses of his large body. Streams of soap rushed around the curves and dripped from Cliff's deliciously carved cliffs. Coby was always transfixed by big guys like Cliff. They had the bodies he could never hope to have. The world didn't have enough growth hormones or steroids for Coby to achieve… *that*. He swallowed nervously as he watched Cliff soap up his (no other way to put it) great big ass. Great. Big. Ass.

"You're flagging."

One of the rugby players—from listening around the fitness center, Coby had learned his name was Seth—passed him by on the way into the shower and pointed at the large outcropping in Coby's shorts.

Coby decided to sit on a bench and wait for Cliff to finish. When Cliff had showered, Coby followed the wet piece of meat to his locker and approached him carefully.

"What do you need, Coby?" Cliff said without granting him so much as eye contact. "Am I going to need to start charging you when I shower? My webcam days are done."

Coby couldn't help but give Cliff another long gratuitous look-over as the big man dried himself off. He wondered how many dicks had been inside of that big bouncing ass. He cleared his throat.

"I hear you're competing now. In bodybuilding, that is."

"Yeah. I'm trying. And?"

Coby drew closer. "Well, you know those guys use the juice, don't you? They use real good stuff. Real heavy-duty stuff from Mexico and Russia."

Cliff looked at him, eyes full of boredom and annoyance.

"What I mean to say is, I can get you some of what they get. I can get it for you for real cheap."

"Are you trying to sell me drugs, Coby? Is that your new career?" Cliff dried his underarms. Every bit of him was swollen. Coby wanted to squeeze him and see if he squeaked.

"What?" Coby laughed. "Career? No…. Well, maybe. The point is, I can get you some real potent stuff. Stuff that will send you right over the top. I just got some new juice in that's freak-inducing. Honest. Monster stuff. And with your size already, combined with this freak juice, you would be unstoppable."

Coby knew he had piqued Cliff's interest. There was that familiar look in the eyes he had seen with countless other muscleheads. Plus, Cliff's dick had become a little hard at the mention of possible monstrosity.

He said nothing, though. He looked to be weighing his options as he got dressed. At least he hadn't yet told Coby to "beat it, kid." Coby hated that. He hated when they called him a kid. He just had to sell the idea a little more. Just one more push.

"Hey, Cliff." Rick appeared behind Coby.

Shit, Coby thought.

"What's going on, guys? Is he bothering you, Cliff?"

Coby smiled innocently at Rick, as if it were a friendly jest.

Cliff smirked. "No. I think we're through."

Damn!

"Well," Coby said, still smiling, "I guess I'll see you later." He didn't know who to direct the statement to. He did know that Rick would not hesitate to call the cops on him, though. He was, after all, the one who had caused Rick to lose an eye. Coby feared constantly that Rick might seek revenge on him one day.

He stepped outside the Hot Body Gym and paced for a minute, having forgotten his gym bag—a literal plastic bag from Walmart—inside in a locker. He needed a big sell. Something huge, or else his debt holders would be coming for him again. Cliff would be an amazing "get" for him. And he would have had him too, if it weren't for Rick. Sweet, unforgiving Rick. The one that got away, though not unscathed.

Seth came out of the fitness center with his bag. He nodded at Coby. It looked to be a bit of a flirtatious nod, so Coby was, at first, confused. He looked behind him and then realized the rugby player was indeed nodding at him. Seth approached Coby with that swagger only men with big thighs can accomplish without looking like cocky assholes. Coby's eyes widened. He felt like he was shrinking.

"Want to go have some fun?" Seth asked. The gaps from his missing teeth made a whistling sound.

"S-sure," Coby unintentionally whistled back.

CASSIE and Vera stood at the door. Cassie held a polite and beautifully designed fruit basket for the new neighbors. They were a strange group, this new "family," but surely they liked fruits. Vera pressed the doorbell for the fifth time with her long acrylic nail. Blood red.

"I do think somebody—plural—is trying to avoid us," she said.

There was scuffling and whispering behind the door. Cassie and Vera looked at one another, knowing they were being watched.

"They're praying us away," Cassie said.

"I hear there has been much ado about this new brood since last we saw them moving in."

"It's true. Just today our beloved Terrence found himself the focus of some divine wrath. The older woman went all kinds of Pentecostal on his boom box."

"Are they Pentecostal?"

"Oh, I don't know, darling. You know they all look the same to me."

"Well, I've had enough of this," Vera said. "Nobody ignores us."

With the basket still in her hands, Cassie followed Vera around the house as they peered through windows.

"Hello," Vera sang loudly. "You have visitors."

"With food," Cassie added.

Soon they realized they were following the new neighbors around their home, chasing movement and shadow from one room to the next.

"Oh, it's a game, Vera! They're playing with us."

"How cute." Vera did not say those words with the least bit of sincerity. "Now, listen, y'all!" she said loudly. "I haven't got time to play. Auntie Vera is a busy woman, so you come on out of there and take your damn fruit."

"Look!" Cassie said. "One of them just darted through the kitchen!"

"You little booger! Get back here."

"I think they're back in the front of the house."

"We ain't leaving until we see somebody," Vera yelled as they made their way around to the front once again. "I don't wear these heels for just anyone, and—oh, hello...."

Michelle stood at the now open front door. Cassie handed the basket to her. "Here you go, dear. We just thought we'd welcome you—"

The door was shut on Cassie's face. Vera's mouth dropped open.

"Uh-uh!" Vera said as she banged on the door. "You don't treat a lady like that. Where are your goddamn manners?"

"It's all right, Vera," Cassie said. "Let's leave them be."

"Leave? No. I'm gonna kick ginger Wednesday's ass."

"As much fun as that might be, we don't want them calling the police."

Vera collected herself. "You're right, of course." She linked arms with Cassie, and they walked away with their heads held high. "Rudeness is inexcusable, though."

"I agree." Cassie looked back at the house. "But before we start a war, we need to size them up. To see who we're up against. I think they might be a bit more trouble than we had originally thought."

LATER that day, after their Bible study and in between prayers (they prayed more than Jehovah's Witnesses circa 1975), Mr. Scott and his tiny congregation discussed their plan as they sat at the dining room table. There was no food before them. Not when the Bible was on the table. The scriptures were the only sustenance they needed, even if their stomachs begged to differ. Mr. Scott once again sat at the head of the table.

"Now," he said, his voice straining to take on some command, "we have at last come to it. On this night we begin the process of cleansing this filth-ridden world. As evidenced by the events of this afternoon—our harassment at the hands of those two *Jezebels*—we have come just in time."

"They should be proud they are among the first to be purified," Newt said. "Ain't that so, Mr. Scott?"

Mr. Scott gave the youth a backhand across the face.

"They should be proud of nothing!" Mr. Scott bellowed. "And don't speak until I am finished. As I was saying, we have a big night ahead of us. A big night filled with... many big... things." He had lost his train of inspiration. "I trust we all know which part we are to play?" He eyed each person at the table individually. "We must not have anything go wrong. Smooth as silk, it must go. Yes, yes."

Sally raised her hand and was acknowledged. "Yes, Sister Sally," Mr. Scott said. "Speak."

Sally cleared her voice as if she was about to give a presentation in front of a large lecture hall filled with strangers. "Thank you, Mr. Scott," she said. Her hands were folded in front of her on the table. "Do we have the electroshock equipment? Has it arrived? Do you know how to use it?"

"No, no, no." Mr. Scott's words tumbled from his mouth like balls down stairs. "Unfortunately, we cannot afford the blessed extravagance of an electroshock machine. It would have certainly made things easier on us, but finances do not presently permit it. If I feel in the future that it is imperative we use one, well then I'm sure we can rig something up. After all, there is electricity all around, isn't there? We may not even need to purchase a machine. We're bright children of God. Perhaps we can make one of our own."

Sally raised her hand and was acknowledged again.

"But what about the money we received from Miss Hench for the congregation? Can't we use that to purchase an electroshock machine?"

"I have invested Miss Hench's kind donation into something I believe—I *know*—will be of much more benefit to the cause. Yes, yes."

"But Mr. Scott," Sally said, her hand still raised, "Miss Hench had specific ideas in mind as to where that money should go. She wanted an electroshock machine to be used."

"Don't question me, Sister!" Mr. Scott raised his voice. "You're obsessed with this electroshock machine. I know what I am doing. Miss Hench will be grateful."

Sally bowed her head. "Yes, Mr. Scott. I'm sorry, Mr. Scott."

Newt cautiously raised his hand.

Mr. Scott rolled his eyes. "Yes, what is it, Brother Newt?"

"I'm hungry, Mr. Scott," said the boy. "We need food."

"The Lord will provide when and how He sees fit. I don't know what more proof you need of that than this very afternoon when those two Jezebels brought us that array of fruits."

Newt brightened. "Can we have some?"

"No. Not now. We must conserve."

"But you had some."

"I was making certain that apple wasn't contaminated with sin, boy!"

"Yes, sir."

"Now, enough chatter. Let us pray."

After the prayer—a long recitation of how unworthy they were of God's love yet still worthier of it than others—everyone was excused. Mr. Scott gently took hold of Michelle's wrist as she passed his chair. She looked down at him with the same apathy she always had since he had found her. Mr. Scott looked around to make certain they were alone. Sally and Newt had gone off to ready themselves for the night to come.

"Do you have what I asked you for, my pretty little girl?" Mr. Scott asked, grinning up at her from beneath his bushy whiskers.

From a large pocket in the front of her dull gown, Michelle pulled out a wadded ball of white cloth. She placed it in his waiting hand.

"Very good," he said, unfolding the used underwear. "This will prove most useful in readjusting our future guests once the aversion therapy begins to work. You may go, Michelle."

She looked back once only to see him sniffing her underwear in what looked like a drug addict's frenzy.

"WELL," Melinda said, her voice quivering slightly, "here we go."

She was dressed very conservatively, as if she was visiting a priest or a nun. They had stopped by her house so she could change before heading back out to see Nanna. Becky had snarked when Melinda came out wearing a black dress with a high neck and a low hem. Melinda hadn't even dressed like that when Nanna was living with her.

Melinda pressed the buzzer located beside the name "Hench." They stood at the bottom of a three-story redbrick walk-up.

"Nice neighborhood," Becky noted.

"Yes," Melinda agreed, looking around. "A steep upgrade from where she last lived."

"How do you think she pays for it?"

Melinda gave Becky a worried look. "I have no idea."

"Yes?" came Nanna's razored voice over the intercom.

"Hi… Mother." She looked to Becky and shrugged. "It's Melinda. Can I come in to see you? We need to talk."

There was a pause.

"I'll meet you down there," the old woman huffed.

The door was buzzed open.

"Does Nanna even know that you know she's not your real mother?"

"No. If she did, we'd have never gotten in. We just need to get into her apartment and find something that might help Bethany and me

53

with our search. Anything at all. The problem is, I don't know what *anything at all* looks like."

The lobby was nice and coordinated, if dimly lit. There were mailboxes to one side and a sitting area with a potted plant to the other. Harmless piano music was piped overhead. There was an older gentleman stationed at a table as some form of security or assurance. Melinda smiled at him. Then she realized he was sleeping and most likely had been since he got the job.

Melinda and Becky waited at the foot of a staircase. A loud mechanical holler of iron and rusty joints punctuated the air. The noise came from the top of the stairs. Melinda started breathing heavily. Then the whirling engine of a stair lift brought into sight the silhouette of Nanna Hench. Melinda got chills. The moment had the promise of becoming something truly cinematic and spine-tingling—the dim lighting, the mechanical squeak of used gears, and the haze of cigarette smoke as Nanna descended toward them. There was initially some heavy tension. If only the ride hadn't taken so damn long. By the time the stair lift stopped in front of them, Melinda was looking at her watch and Becky was yawning.

Nanna stood from the stair lift, dressed in a navy blue business suit. She looked different. Her demeanor was more businesslike than Melinda had ever seen. She folded her arms. Her skinny cigarette was held high by two skinny fingers. Nanna looked Melinda once over. She ignored Becky altogether.

"Mother," Melinda said, offering a smile. "You smoke?"

Nanna avoided answering the obvious. "Why is *she* here?" She finally looked accusingly at Becky.

"Because I just love visiting mean little old ladies. When Melinda told me she was coming, I asked if I could come along."

Melinda cut through the tension. "We're just out for a drive. We passed your lovely new home and decided we'd drop in."

Nanna laughed. It woke the security guard. "Don't lie to me, missy. I may not be part of your life anymore, but I still know you better than anyone."

"Why don't we go talk in your apartment? There are some things I need to say."

Nanna gave her a suspicious glare and blew out a column of smoke. "Where are your manners? You don't just invite yourself into other people's homes. No wonder Patrick turned out the way he did."

"You leave Patrick alone." Melinda's face had lost all kindness. "He's turned out just fine."

"No. The only boy on Jasper Lane to turn out any good, the only one to atone for his sinful behavior, is Jason Bloom. He's the boy Patrick should have been. Despite his mother, Jason has become a good God-fearing boy. He would have made his grandma proud."

Melinda and Becky exchanged puzzled glances.

"How do you know Jason Bloom?" Melinda asked.

Nanna flicked her cigarette. "He came to see me a while back. Said he was going to get right with God. He knew I could help him, you see. He knew who to come to. He's out of the grips of that trashy mother of his and now counseling at a camp that specializes in—"

She stopped when she noticed the intensity with which Melinda and Becky were listening to her.

"Where is this camp?" Becky said. "What's it called?"

Nanna pursed her dry lips, then sat back down in the stair lift and buckled herself in. "You'll get no more out of me," she said. "I've said too much as it is. I'm an old fool for playing into your trick."

The stair lift started to slowly climb back up the stairs.

"Wait," Melinda said. "Mother, there are things you have to tell me."

"Nothing!" Nanna hissed. "I have to tell you nothing! Ever again." She threw her cigarette in the direction of the guard. "Horace! Get these ladies out of here."

"Mother!" Melinda shouted in anger.

"You know," Becky said to Nanna, "the two of us can easily overpower any moving thing that is currently in this room."

Horace shuffled over to Melinda and Becky. "Don't make me get rough," he said.

"Come on, Mel," Becky said with a roll of her eyes. "We'll get your bitch mother later."

As they left, the stair lift had stalled halfway up the staircase and Nanna was trying to shake it back to life.

"What a wasted trip!" Melinda said with a stomp of her foot when she and Becky were back out on the street. "She makes me furious."

"It wasn't a wasted trip at all." Becky hooked her arm under Melinda's. "At least now we know where Jason is."

DAVID was in bed, washing down his sleeping pill with a glass of water.

"Are you coming to bed soon?" he asked Cliff.

Cliff had just changed into a small pair of retro-styled blue boxer briefs made to resemble high school gym shorts. They fit him snugly. He wasn't wearing a shirt.

"I'll be there in a minute," he answered. "I'm going to have my muffin first."

David, of course, had just had *his* nightly muffin. His face had just been buried deep in Cliff's ass for half an hour. His tongue had done some major spelunking, and as usual, he'd had to come up for air on more than one occasion or risk being smothered by Cliff's tremendous loaves of butt.

"Things will work out," David assured his husband. "You'll be Mr. Universe in no time."

Cliff smiled. "Go to sleep, baby. I'll be back up in a few minutes."

He grabbed a bran muffin from the kitchen and walked lazily onto the front porch. He preferred to leave the porch light off when he was having his muffin at night. The darkness soothed him, calmed him, and readied him for bed. The fall night air was chilly. He absentmindedly played with his nipples as he stood on the porch, running his palm over them and tweaking their hard tips as he took a healthy bite from the muffin.

Out of nowhere, it seemed, the small form of a young woman appeared on the walkway in front of the porch. She stood there and stared. Cliff recognized her unkempt long mess of hair as that belonging to Michelle of the Crazies.

"Um...," Cliff said. "Can I help you?"

She said nothing.

Before he could ask anything more, there was a sudden rush around him. He was tackled from behind. Sally jumped on him, wrapping her legs around his waist and shoving a chloroformed rag over his nose and mouth. To his sides, Mr. Scott and Newt came at him to keep his arms from knocking Sally away. There was a struggle, but soon Cliff was overcome. He fell backward and right on top of Sally, who gasped with a stifled cry. Mr. Scott tried to help her, but the unconscious giant then fell over onto him. Newt came to Mr. Scott's aid, and Cliff then flattened *him*. It continued like this for longer than it should have, until Michelle finally tired of watching the spoof of a kidnapping and got everything under control. They each took an appendage and, as inconspicuously as was possible, carried Cliff to their home.

The Chapter in Which Cliff Wakes Up in a Basement

DAVID awoke alone the next morning. Cliff, who was always a ridiculously clingy sleeper, was not there to unwrap from. (It was usually akin to sleeping next to a shaved bear.) This was not strange in and of itself. Oftentimes Cliff got up early for a morning run or an early workout while David was still asleep. But this morning it looked as if Cliff's side of the bed had not been slept in at all.

David rubbed his eyes and walked downstairs in his boxer shorts, checking through the house for his husband. The kitchen light was on, but there was no bodybuilder in sight. Cliff would never have left the light on. He had been trained by David to conserve energy. He had even agreed to get rid of his big angry Hummer for a more practical Jeep. A Jeep that, as David stepped onto the front porch in the cool morning air, he noticed was still in the drive.

David hugged himself, getting a chill from the slight nip in the air. It looked to be a beautiful day, but there was something different about it, some edge to it. Then David noticed the bran muffin scattered in bits all over the porch. He ran back into the house and pulled on a hoodie before heading over to Terrence's place.

Terrence had visitors. There was an extra car in the driveway. The queens had arrived en masse. David pictured them piling out of the vehicle like clowns in a circus. Terrence was in his backyard with the cheerful visitors. The Mean Girls were already at full cat. They were dressed—nay, *doused*—in militant pink. Shorts, jackets, caps—everything as pink as a little girl's dream, and the queens were dancing to music coming from Terrence's stereo system inside the house. Terrence was standing at the patio table, mixing bright-pink paint into a large bucket.

"Davey!" he said on seeing David. "Just in time. We need the muscle. Would you like to help us in our revenge against Sally Trolls?"

The Mean Girls hooted and hollered at the sight of David in his boxers.

"I don't even want to know what you are up to," David said. "Have any of you seen Cliff this morning? Maybe jogging past your art class here?"

"Sorry, hon," Terrence said. "We've been busy all morning here in back. We're going to go give Silly Sally and her freaky family a little paint job."

He got a roar of support from the queens.

"I'm sure Cliff will show up," Terrence continued. "He's probably just doing something muscle-y. Lifting a building or flexing for someone somewhere. You know how he loves to do that."

David nodded, though clearly less than certain.

Terrence put aside the paint for a moment. "Listen," he said. "When I'm through here, I'll help you look for him, okay? And then you must let me spank him."

"And me!" chimed a Mean Girl.

"And me!" said another.

"Me too!" said a third.

"Thanks, Terry."

"No problem, babe. Are you sure you don't want to come with us? You'd be supporting the arts."

"No. You go ahead. I'll watch from a safe distance."

"All right, then," Terrence said, straightening his cap. He picked up the bucket of paint. "Come on, ladies. We got a cross to decorate."

David stood aside as the flood of pink surged past him. He only watched for a moment as the group loudly made their way to the Jones's old home and its new lawn ornament. He headed back to his own house without waiting to see the commotion that was sure to occur.

Maybe it was silly, but David was worried. Cliff had never gone anywhere without at least leaving a note. This was most peculiar. It left a knot in David's stomach. He missed his morning kiss.

CLIFF woke from a fog and knew at once the mattress he was lying on was not his own. It felt damp and smelled old, and there was an uncomfortable lump poking his lower back. He was in a basement. That much was certain. The small basement windows were covered with cardboard, and from what he could see, there was little else around him other than an old television on a stand located at his feet.

His hands were chained to the wall and his feet secured to hooks on the floor. In his mouth was, of all things, a ball gag. The thought came to him that perhaps David was playing some kinky game, but that was, of course, silly. David would not have knocked him out if he wanted to play. He would have given Cliff poppers so that he would play harder.

Though hazy, Cliff slowly began to piece together the attack from the night before. He remembered seeing Michelle on the sidewalk and then feeling someone jump him from behind.

He tried to free himself from the restraints, but it was of no use. Whoever these magic Christians really were, they had him good. He was nearly naked and completely vulnerable in someone else's basement. Were they going to stone him? Was that what biblical literalists did?

The door to the basement opened, and down into the dim room came a figure. The overhead light danced on, and there stood Mr. Scott dressed in a suit of white and looking like Colonel Sanders's serial-killer twin brother. Only not as well fed.

"You can't escape, young man," Mr. Scott said bluntly. "And honestly this is for your own good, so just relax."

Cliff gave the old man a look of extreme contempt. He growled past the ball gag. He recognized where he was now. This was Steve and Sandy's basement, or what was *once* their basement before they had moved. Cliff had even shot a threesome scene down here for one of his best-selling titles, a sadistic little piece called *The Silence of the Gams*. He wondered if the ball gag he was now sucking on was the same one he'd used in the film. Had Steve left the props behind? Would the titty clamps be put to use again as well? Or the megadildo?

"Growl all you want," Mr. Scott said. "No one will hear you. No, no. For all your precious homosexual lover knows, you left him for another man. You are so promiscuous that it is utterly believable. Yes. Quite so. But you see, that's what I am here to fix. That is my calling on this earth."

He came near Cliff. Mr. Scott was excited. Cliff could see that clearly enough through the white slacks as the old man stood over him.

"You are the first to be set right. To be set right with God. Back on the path, you see. Back on that narrow path leading to everlasting glory. Don't you want the Lord to smile on you again? Wouldn't that be...."

His eyes were drifting over Cliff's mostly naked frame. He was breathing heavily, exerting energy in some unseen way. Slowly, he bent over, his fingers stretching out to touch Cliff's chest. But then someone else came down the stairs. Mr. Scott, for lack of a better word, *straightened* up immediately.

The dowdy older woman came and stood beside Mr. Scott, looking down at Cliff in a manner not dissimilar to the old man's. Her eyes were wider, though. More in awe.

"Sister Sally here will feed you. The piss pot is there beside your bed. Brother Newt will come down and help you with... those matters."

"You'll appreciate this," Sally said, her eyes never losing their apoplectic stare. "You'll see. It will be *wonderful*."

"In the meantime," Mr. Scott said as he turned on the small television at Cliff's feet, "we will get started on your treatment immediately. No time to waste. No time like the present. No, sir."

The television had no sound and two of its dials were missing, but it was hooked up to an old VCR. The screen flashed one image after another of beautiful, curvy women. It was an older video, and Cliff imagined it would have a routine porn score if he could hear it. Though lacking any real diversity—all the women were as white as salt—the one thing the video did offer was a surprising amount of boobs. Cliff rolled his eyes at this obvious attempt at some type of aversion therapy. Maybe if he sprouted a boner they would just let him go, thinking that they had done their job well. *Look! He's got a boner! He's cured! Hallelujah!*

There was a loud commotion overhead, and a third individual came down the stairs. "Pink!" Newt yelled. "That funny man and his ugly lady friends are painting the cross pink, Mr. Scott!"

Mr. Scott and Sally gasped and skittered away, leaving Cliff alone at once. The light was turned out so that Cliff was in the dark with the television and its boobies. He could hear hollering outside, but only faintly. It was most definitely Terrence. Cliff hoped he was giving Mr. Scott and Norma Desperate more trouble than they could handle. That would give him time to figure a way out of his nightmarish predicament. Away from the closeted self-loather and his weird little clan. Away from—

Oh, Lord! Vagina! This video has vagina! What type of Christian video shoves muff in your face?

IF HER mind had been on it, Cassie would have been laughing something fierce as Terrence and the Mean Girls doused the large cross in the Jones's yard with a bucket of bright pink paint. She watched everything from the front patio of her house with Melinda and Vera, but her reaction was restrained. Melinda would certainly have gasped at the same sight. Yet since the previous evening, when Melinda had brought Cassie the news of where Jason had been for weeks, both ladies found it hard to concentrate on anything. Melinda looked like misery for having had such news to tell. They watched the proceedings below with only minimal interest, perhaps as something to store later for comment and critique.

"This camp where Jason is staying," Melinda said with interest, "it's a bad place?"

"Straight To The Heart?" Cassie replied. "It's just awful. I don't know why he would go there. I hope he's not actually trying to change who he is. I hope their lies haven't found a way into his head."

Vera put her hand over Cassie's in comfort.

"His father wanted to send him there," Cassie continued. "To straighten him out. What a ridiculous idea. But his father was a ridiculous man. He deserved what he got...." She quieted herself, realizing, nearly too late, that Melinda had no idea what had truly happened to Jackson Bloom. "Or whatever got him."

"One of *those* camps?" Melinda spoke with shock. "I was hoping they weren't real. That they were some made-up haunted house story."

"They're real. Any horrible thing the human mind can think of is real. All an idea needs is a twisted monster behind it pulling the strings. Yes. They're very real and very dangerous."

There was no drinking this morning. No alcohol, anyway. The ladies had coffees, and that was all.

"You're going to go get him, aren't you?" Vera asked.

"I am indeed."

"What?" Melinda seemed surprised. "How? Are you just going to march in the camp and force Jason to come home with you? He's a grown man, Cassie. They probably have guards, and those guards most likely expect trouble."

"They haven't seen *this* trouble. Wouldn't you do the same thing if Patrick were in a similar situation?"

Melinda had nothing to say to that.

"You know you would. There is overprotection and underprotection. The trick is knowing which extreme to side with when extremes are called for. I don't want my son to be any more hurt by life than he has been. I can see his scars as clear as day."

"I'd go with you, sweetie," Vera offered, "but the club needs me so near to the holiday." (Meaning Halloween, of course.)

"I appreciate it, but I can do this alone."

Below, Terrence and the Mean Girls were making a retreat. Mr. Scott and Sally were howling around the cross as if Christ himself was on it.

"When are you heading out?" Melinda asked.

"Tomorrow. I think tomorrow would be good. It's time to put all this worry behind me. I need to know what the hell my son is doing at a place like that. And I need to prepare myself for his answer."

DAVID did everything short of getting the police involved in his search for Cliff. Having the police on Jasper Lane again was not a good idea, especially with the history of the place and the rather large secrets of its residents. There was, after all, a murder that David himself had helped cover up. Besides, it was still too early for the police to do anything. A person had to be missing for a certain number of hours before squad cars and dogs could be called. David knew—he just *knew*—something was wrong, though. Cliff never just disappeared like this without a word, and the thought that Cliff would ever leave him for another man was... too much. Not ridiculous, but definitely too much.

David had called their friends and family, but no one had heard anything from Cliff. He tried his best not to sound an alarm when talking to Cliff's reactionary father, a man who saw conspiracy with the change in weather. That was a tightrope, but he succeeded in the end.

He knew he could count on his closest friends—those who did not have their own impending disasters—to help him out in his search. Terrence, paint-spattered and avenged, went door-to-door with Becky, asking anyone if they had seen Cliff. They even had a photograph of the hulking behemoth. Surely no one would have missed seeing him. But block after block, they came up empty-handed.

David stayed back at the house, calling everyone on his and Cliff's cell phones. He realized that he might seem desperate—that he might look like a boy overreacting—but this was Cliff, and Cliff was part of him. One did not simply wake up missing a limb and hope it returned on its own sometime during the day.

James and Rick drove into town. They searched the health stores and the gyms and the places Cliff liked to shop for his impossibly tight clothes. They called the fitness center to ask if anyone had seen him. No one had. There was a more hardcore fitness center in town where Cliff worked out among other bodybuilders on occasion, so they hit that. It was called Shred Headz. When they did not find him there, they headed back to Hot Body Gym to look for the big guy themselves.

"He's not here," James said after having checked the showers. Rick was at the front desk, scanning the gym with his cycloptic vision. "Seth and your ex, Coby, are getting to know each other pretty well in the locker room, though. You might want to keep an eye on that situation."

"How sweet," Rick said. "They've bonded over their mutual lust for me."

"Yeah." James started to laugh but then suddenly didn't find the thought very amusing. He realized that it was likely the truth.

Coach Nipple was at the hack squat (a rudely named machine if there ever was one) with a couple of his wrestlers. The coach looked ever the proud father as he watched over his boys while they trained.

"Nips," James said, approaching the hack squat, "have you seen Cliff in here today?"

"Hey, guys," the coach responded. "Nope. I sure haven't, fella. Is everything okay?"

"Most likely," Rick said. "We're just making sure. Cliff's disappeared on everyone."

"Just vanished?"

"Poof."

"You're good friends to take time out of your days to help look for him. That's something I try to instill in my guys on the wrestling team. Good old-fashioned loyalty."

James shrugged. "We don't mind. Cliff's a great guy. He's probably fine, but we want to alleviate some of David's worry. Besides, I've really got nothing else to do until rugby starts, and this keeps me busy."

"You know," the coach said, an idea etched into his tone, "I need some help with the team. We have a big meet upstate tomorrow, and my assistant can't make it. Some bullshit about taxes or taxidermy. Maybe it was Texas. Anyway, would you like to come? I mean, I can't promise a good time, but... ah, hell! Yes, I can. It's a wrestling match! We're going to have a blast."

James looked at Rick, who smiled and nodded.

"That sounds like a great time," James said.

"Fantastic! And who knows? That assistant's position might even open up if you'd like to throw your hat in the wrestling ring. Do you know anything about wrestling?"

"I did a bit of it in the army."

"I *bet* you did, you stud."

Rick leaned in to Coach Nipple and said, "Thank you! I mean that emphatically. *Thank you.*"

"I've been so damn bored," said James. "*So* damn bored."

"Though," Rick said to James as an aside just between the two of them, "you realize you could just be trading one form of porn for another."

The two wrestlers had completely chucked their training and instead groped and played with one another in jest, completely oblivious to the coach, James, and Rick.

"Guys!" Coach Nipple yelled. "Get back to it. Stop being distractions."

COBY and Seth sat up beside each other in the bed after a rather rousing game of Rabbit in the Hole. It was a surprise for Coby to find himself in the sack with the rugby player again, but after being discovered frolicking in the Hot Body Gym showers, what else were they supposed to do? They simply *had* to find a bed. It would have been unhealthy for both of them to suppress what had been building up just before James—*damn that James for so many things!*—walked in on them. James would certainly tell Rick, and Coby had been warned by Rick before that if he was caught rubbing his dick on anyone in the showers ever again, he would be denied membership. Then how would he be able to get to Cliff?

So Coby and Seth slipped out of the fitness center and found some seedy motel called Cheap Rooms For Cheap (at least they were honest) in which to finish their play. It wasn't the worst place Coby had ever been. In his dealings with those he dealt with, he'd seen seedier. Still, there were stains on the bed cover that might have been from any number of bodily secretions, and the shower looked a strange shade of light green. Like moldy mint.

Coby had thought his fun with Seth was a one-time thing, but here they were again, and Coby could barely wrap his legs around Mr. Rugby. Seth was bigger and bulkier than the guys Coby usually messed around with. Most of those guys were not active sportsmen. Sometimes they were so high they weren't active *anything*.

Seth was also an extremely hairy man. Coby had never seen an ass with as much hair on it, and strangely enough he found the bearded bum very sexy. He also found himself encouraging the roughness of Seth's sex play. It hurt. It hurt a great deal. But Coby not only desired the pain but found it comforting. When they were done, it took a good five minutes for either of them to regain their breath.

"You deal drugs?" Seth asked in a nonchalant manner. "Steroids and shit?"

This was the most probing conversation yet between them.

"Yeah. Do you want some? I got some pot." Coby pointed to his gym bag on the old scuffed table by the window.

"No. I don't do that stuff. Well, 'roids maybe. But only a little. Not enough to get in trouble or shrink my balls. And never in season. People want me off the team for enough reasons already without me getting caught juicing. I have to be smart about things."

"You're still playing? I thought you had quit."

Seth looked at him. Coby wondered if he had said something stupid. Or something that was going to get him fucked comatose. The looks were not dissimilar. "I quit for a week a while back. But I love playing, so I crawled back, tail between my legs."

"Why did you quit?"

Seth didn't answer the question. "How do you know Cliff?" he asked instead. "You must know him well to approach him about steroids."

"Not really. He's friends with my ex, Rick."

Suddenly Coby noticed Seth's eyes—his entire grumpy face—light up.

"You know Rick?" Seth asked.

"Yeah. Yeah. I know Rick."

Seth was looking at Coby again with a lusty stare. His dick, a thick beaten-up troll of a thing complete with drool, stiffened once more.

"Tell me about him," Seth said.

Coby knew what this was. He knew he was acting as a substitute for someone else. For Rick. But it was sex, after all, and Seth wanted him bad at the moment. So Coby grinned and gave in to his own desire.

Still, he thought, *it would be nice for someone just once to look at me like that and mean it.*

SuburbaNights: Vignettes from Jasper Lane

WHEN Melinda told of the nightmare the following day, she blamed it on Coach Malcolm Nipple. She had been sleeping very well of late. She didn't even need any sleeping meds like everyone else she knew. It helped that she had always imagined herself as Sleeping Beauty. In a meditative state, she saw her body perfectly still, her skin flawless and porcelain, and a slight smile ever on her rose-red lips as she slept in her expensive sheets and silk nightgown. When she woke up, she tried, and very often managed, to greet the day with a smile, as if at any moment she could break out in song and blue jays would land on her finger.

Of course, if that ever actually happened, she would run to the bathroom and scrub her hands raw with soap. Birds were filthy creatures!

But this night she had barely been to sleep for an hour when she had had the most awful nightmare. Of course, the coach couldn't take all the blame. Nanna had a starring role in the dream, after all. Nanna was a given as the root cause of all of Melinda's nightmares. But the coach? That very afternoon Melinda had been sent a chocolate bouquet from Coach Nipple in one of his endless attempts to regain her affections. She had snacked on a couple of those chocolate delights just an hour before bed. She knew better, but they were so inviting. Just like Coach Malcolm Nipple.

The nightmare began, from what Melinda could remember, with Nanna Hench showing up at the front door. She looked as disapproving as ever, her sagging face the lone aspect of the old woman Melinda could see in the dream.

"Mother," Melinda said in a voice that sang. In the nightmare she was privy to her own image as well... *and she looked fabulous!* She wore a diamond tiara in her elegantly curled hair, and an elegant white satin evening gown. "What are you doing here?" She spoke softly, innocently, like a fairy-tale princess.

"I know what you know!" hollered Nanna.

Hand to the heart. Eyes wide. "Whatever do you mean?"

Behind Nanna, bright lights flooded the street. Suddenly there was a camera crew and a large crowd of onlookers. Melinda recognized

69

some of her friends' faces in the crowd, but there were many strangers as well. They rushed at the house. Police cruisers pulled into the drive.

"The fuzz!" Nanna bellowed.

She pushed her way past Melinda and into the house. She grabbed hold of Melinda's arm.

"They'll never take me alive!" the old woman cried.

Melinda was terrified. Nanna had begun to change right before her eyes, to take the form of some curious woodland creature. A badger or something equally vicious. A lemur, maybe? Melinda didn't know animals or their ratings on the viciousness scale, but she knew animal transformations were rarely good things. However, what frightened her more than the now snarling Nanna-beast was the fact that outside her door were not only reporters but a reality TV crew as well, who were broadcasting this whole mess to the world. Melinda screamed.

"Mother, no! Not *COPS*! Let us not fall that low. Just give yourself up! Please!"

But Nanna didn't respond. She growled. At once, Melinda saw herself as a petite white mouse over which the Nanna-beast towered. Nanna the badger/lemur hunched her shoulders, ready to jump on Melinda and eat her whole.

She squeaked in fear. "No! Don't eat me!"

That was when the front door burst open and in rushed Cassie Bloom with the police in tow.

"There she is!" Cassie said.

The police grabbed Nanna and shoved her furry little body into a brown burlap sack even as she hissed and barked. Melinda breathed a mousy sigh of relief, most grateful to her dear friend Cassie.

"Now," Cassie said, looking down at Melinda, "what do we do with this one?"

"It's me!" Melinda squeaked. "It's your friend Melinda Gold!"

"Exterminator!" Cassie yelled. "We've got a mouse problem."

Melinda woke up from the nightmare not feeling at all fresh and pretty. In fact, she felt rather sweaty. Like a man probably felt all the time. She gave herself a minute to calm down and then reached for the phone. She dialed Cassie, holding a hand over her chest to feel her heart.

"Do you have room for me tomorrow?" she asked before Cassie had even said a word.

"Melinda?" Cassie replied in a confused waking voice.

"To find Jason. Is there room for me in the car tomorrow when you head out to find your son?"

"Of course. But… why?"

"Well, honestly, there are two reasons. I'm feeling a little responsible for all of this, and if there's a chance my mother is involved in this camp, there might also be information on her there. Maybe something that could lead me to my real mother. I would like to come if there is room."

"There's plenty of room, darling," Cassie said. "And… thank you. For offering to come along. It means a lot. Maybe we'll both find some answers to our questions."

"Good," Melinda said. She said good night and hung up the phone.

"Good," she repeated to herself.

CLIFF found himself dozing off. Only the flashes of the pervy Christian porn video kept him from getting any real sleep. He had spent the day looking around the basement as best he could for some means of escape. The video was really too much. Aversion therapy indeed. He averted his eyes from the screen. He never wanted to see another pair of female breasts in his life, and if he ever did decide to do porn again, they could forget about any bisexual scenes.

Eric Arvin

Earlier that day there had been once when he thought he might have had a chance to get away. That was when Newt had come down to help him with bathroom matters. However, one of Cliff's hands had been kept tied to the wall at all times, making things more difficult. Still, escape was not out of the question. But the skittish little bastard had a gun. Cliff did not want to get shot, so he played it cool and hoped for another opportunity. He even remained quiet when the ball gag was removed from his mouth. It was best to play down his bigness if at all possible. He'd keep thinking. There had to be a way out.

He knew David was looking for him. Terrence too. But how would Cliff alert them to his location? God, he missed David. He missed holding him so much that it ached in the way that characters in plays always said it did, and they had only been apart one day. He couldn't even imagine how much worse that longing would get. Would it drive him crazy?

The basement door latch unlocked and someone entered the darkness, leaving the light off. They descended the stairs in cautious steps. Just before the television was turned off, Cliff saw the mousy face of Sister Sally.

She edged closer to him.

"You don't need that nasty video," she whispered. She was getting too close. Cliff could see the glassiness in her eyes and heard the anxious excitement in her breath. "You can have me instead. I offer myself to you. It's God's will. He wants you to ravish me!"

HOLY. FUCK.

She was straddling him, rubbing her unmoisturized hands all over his well-groomed muscles, and like Mr. Scott, she was seemingly starved for something she could not have. Her breathing was like a wet black blanket.

"I need... I need you to be inside of me," she went on. "It's what the Lord wants. I know it. I thought he wanted me to be alone. To dry up serving him. But now I see the truth. He just wanted me to wait. He was bringing you to me. Oh, thank you, Lord!"

72

Cliff could do nothing but squirm. He tried to will his wiener to shrink up inside abdomen. If only....

The television flashed back on suddenly, and Sally shrieked as she looked over her shoulder. There stood Michelle, watching them in tired disinterest. Sally leaped from Cliff at once and ran up the stairs, shielding her face and praying. Michelle stood still and eyed Cliff for a little while longer. Cliff wanted to thank her, but of course, there was that ball gag in his mouth making it impossible.

She approached him slowly and then, without pause, smacked him so hard across the face that it stung deep. There was a glint of satisfaction in her eyes. Then she too went upstairs.

David. Hurry. These bitches is crazy!

DAVID sat on the porch with the light off, hoping Cliff might return from wherever he had gone off to. That he would show up and say that he'd only gone for a jog and had gotten lost. That he had spent the day helping the new family move in some old furniture. That he had won some spontaneous bodybuilding expo and had spent the day touring and enjoying the trappings of fame. Anything. David knew he was not going to be getting any real sleep until Cliff came home. He'd be a wreck until then, an unshaven wreck.

As he sat there, the porch filled up. Gayhound came and sat beside him, offering his unconditional love. Terrence walked over to be with him. Becky, Rick, and James—they all came over to lend their support. To wait. They were mostly silent.

"We'll find him, babes," Terrence said. "Don't you worry."

The Chapter in Which Licorice Whips Fall into Ill Repute

THE next morning Terrence had the Mean Girls searching for miles around for any sign of Cliff. They hung posters of Cliff on telephone poles and in grocery stores. In some of these, the former porn star was in what might be considered indecent poses. In fact, one of the posters was simply a photo of Cliff's famous ass. Since Cliff was most probably not walking around with both cheeks hanging out, even Terrence didn't see the point to that particular sheet.

"I'll save it, though," he said, rolling it up tightly. "You never know when it might come in… handy."

Terrence and David stayed near the house as the Mean Girls canvassed the area. Always "just in case." They walked back and forth along the sidewalk in front of the house, each with his cell phone ready. The neighbors passed, offering their support. They were all there for David. Of course David appreciated it, but his mind was a flurry of active *what ifs*. A flurry that was dangerously approaching a blizzard.

"Do you think he left me?" he asked Terrence as they walked. It was the first time he had seriously pondered the idea. "Have I bored him to the point he no longer wants to be with me?"

"You silly bitch. He didn't leave you. You two are the most annoyingly romantic and happy pair of homos I've ever met. Really. It's kind of infuriating."

"If he didn't leave me, then where is he? That would almost be a relief compared to the other possibilities."

"Don't think on those. You're overreacting. That's my job."

"God! What if he's been attacked somewhere? What if he's hurt?"

"David, Cliff is a big boy. A big, big boy. It would take a whole gang of homophobes to bring him down."

"That doesn't exactly make me feel any better. There *are* whole gangs of homophobes out there. They hold office."

They stood at the corner by the stop sign.

"Did Cliff say or do anything before he went missing?" Terrence asked. "Anything strange?"

"Not really. He's just been stressed out, wondering if quitting porn was a good idea. I should have listened more closely."

"Well, I could have answered that for him: *No.* He should have thought of all the great ass shots still left unfilmed. He should have thought of his fans."

They started walking back to David's house.

"Is there anyone we haven't asked if they've seen him?" David wondered. "Anyone who…."

He stopped talking at the sight of Michelle of the Crazies. She was watching them from beside the multicolored cross in her yard. Her nest of red hair was trying to dance in the breeze. Her gaze was fixed and hard.

"You want some more of this?" Terrence shouted at her with attitude. "I got a spackle with your name on it."

"Did you and Becky go to their house yesterday?" David asked him, keeping his eyes on Michelle.

"Hell no. Those creepy assholes might have shot us after we gave their lives some needed color. Anyway, do you think they would tell you if they had seen Cliff? I doubt that."

"They probably wouldn't even open the door to me if I knocked. Still, there is always a chance. The girl, Michelle, she looks fed up with… something."

"Something like life? Existing? Taste?"

"Something like that. I might need to head over there this afternoon after we hear back from your squad just to be sure."

"Well, you be careful, Davey. Maybe you could take Asha along with you. It never hurts to have a little extra protection when dealing with the unbalanced."

"I deal with you fine, don't I?"

"Well, looky there!" Terrence gave David a pleasantly shocked look. "You made a joke at my expense. *Bitch*. You *must* know everything is going to be fine."

THE dusty-blue Cadillac convertible was ready to go. The oil had been checked and the tires rotated. Cassie had no idea what rotating tires meant, but she had it done anyway. Any time anyone she knew had taken a trip, they'd made sure to rotate their tires. Cassie hadn't driven any great distance from Jasper Lane since Jackson bit it, and she was understandably nervous about the whole trip. The convertible hadn't been used in quite a while, so "checking under the hood" sounded wise. When she did drive into town, instead of the Cadillac, Cassie opted for a smaller but no less classy vehicle. This vehicle changed every year.

"All your things are in the trunk," Vera said as she and Cassie stood by the old car. "Make sure you give me updates. I want to know everything that's going on as if I was right there with you."

"I will, darling."

Cassie's attention was drawn to Melinda, who was coming up the drive with surprisingly little luggage—a bag and a retro pink suitcase. Cassie had been expecting they would need to make a few trips into Melinda's house to get everything she wanted to bring.

"Melinda! I was planning to stop by and pick you up. You didn't need to walk all the way up here."

Melinda looked at the Caddy in awe.

"Would you like a napkin for your drool?" Vera teased.

"Where have you been keeping *this*?" Melinda asked, rounding the car as if it might be too hot to touch. "It's beautiful! I've never seen you drive this before. It can't be new."

"It's just one of the many things I have stored away." Cassie spoke with disinterest, as if the Caddy were something she could not figure out what to do with, something destined to be always in the way. Like a piece-of-crap gift from a best friend.

Melinda shook her head in disbelief. "We should go through your stored things when we get back." She put her bag and suitcase in the backseat and then slid into the front, where she gave a sigh of contentment. "Can we leave the top down?"

"It's getting a little chilly for that, don't you think?"

"Please."

Melinda looked so pleading that Cassie could not say no.

"Oh, let her have her way, Mommy," Vera said. "Look at that face."

"We'll be back soon," Cassie said to Vera, and they exchanged kisses. "With Jason."

"Drive safe," Vera said as Cassie got into the Caddy and started the car.

"When have I ever done that?"

"Thatta girl!"

Cassie looked at Melinda. "Are you ready to go, Butch?" she said.

"Butch? Me? I hardly think I'm butch. If I were gay at all, I'd be more along the lines of lipstick lesbian. I think that's what they're called, right? The pretty ones who wear nice clothes. But I would never be butch."

"I was referencing Butch Cassidy, as in *Butch Cassidy and the Sundance Kid*. As in a buddy movie."

"Oh." Pause. "But they were outlaws, Cassie."

"Indeed they were."

77

RICK watched the school van—the one filled with Coach Nipple and his wrestling team—pull into the driveway. He could hear it a block before that. You would have thought they were on their way to a spring break free-for-all, the way they carried on. Hoots and hollers and woots to high heaven. There was either a wrestling match happening in the back of that van or some hard and heavy bromancing. The horn blasted at the house.

"Your ride is here," Rick yelled to James.

James came rushing into the living room. "They're early! I'm not finished packing yet."

"I don't think they care. You better get a move on. They're just going to get louder."

"Shit!" James cursed as he ran back upstairs.

Rick took a drink from his hot tea as he continued to watch out the window. The van was rocking back and forth so hard it looked as if the whole thing might fall apart at any moment. How many little monkeys were jumping on the bed, he wondered. How long could so much testosterone be contained in such a confined space? Rick imagined this was just what James needed, this getaway with guys more like him. Guys whose socks didn't always match. Guys who liked sports scores and action films. And there was a possible new job to be had as well.

He heard James rushing around above him, cursing and fumbling here and there, until at last he made it to the top of the stairs. He did his traditional pause and pat-down, checking for his keys and wallet and trying to remember if he had forgotten anything else. Then he raced down the steps and nearly collided with Rick.

"I'll give you a call," he said, then gave Rick a quick peck on the cheek.

But as quick as he moved, he was not quick enough for that van full of testosterone monsters. Without so much as a knock, they came rushing into the house, a boisterous and cheering group of harmless marauders, grabbed James by the arms, and took his bag.

"Sorry," one of them—the biggest—said to Rick. James was laughing as they carried him away. "We gotta go. We'll make sure he calls you when we get there."

"Take him away," Rick said. "You all have fun."

They cheered in response as they took James to the van. He was but a stick in a wild muscular current. Coach Nipple waved at Rick from the driver's seat. Rick smiled and waved back. Once everyone was in the van—more or less—the coach backed out of the drive and peeled off. Who was actually in control of the situation—the coach or the wrestlers—was anyone's guess.

No sooner had the van sped away than Rick's front door was nearly torn from its hinges once more, but this time by Terrence.

"What was *that*?" he said, breathing heavily. "Those were wrestlers, weren't they? Where are they? I heard them. I saw them. What did you do with them, you selfish shellfish?"

"You missed them," Rick said. "They were all right here, within touching distance. And you missed them."

"Dammit! And I even ran over here."

"I know. I saw you clearing the hedges. You're quick. But they're young."

UPON approach, David noticed how drab and lifeless Steve and Sandy's old house now looked. In only a little time, it had gone from being a bustling place of midday activity to something kids might avoid for fear of the mean family living within its walls. This was now a place that offered no welcome. There was no color. The lawn was not kept up. The drive was not swept. The clunky "family" station wagon was kept in the garage, and the garage door was closed. Every window of the house was now draped over or shuttered. Only the large cross in the front yard offered any real vitality, and that was because of Terrence's spattered pink paint job.

David felt a twinge of sadness. This house was once so much fun. Now? Now it only offered suspicion and judgment.

He rang the doorbell. Nothing. He knocked on the door. Nothing. Undeterred, he waited a minute and knocked again. And again. With every knock and every ring of the doorbell, he became more adamant, more irritated, and more certain of his suspicions. He could hear someone moving about inside. Finally, he called out, "I can wait all day!"

With that the door opened to the older woman, Sally. Her face was tight and irritated. "You get!" she said. "You get off our porch right now!"

She made a movement as if she meant to sweep him off the porch with an invisible broom.

Behind her, positioned in the hallway like models in a painting, were the stoic forms of Michelle and, momentarily, Newt. However, Newt, upon seeing David standing at the door, sprinted off.

"I need to ask you some questions." David calmed down. "My husband is missing and—"

"Husband?" Sally hissed and cackled. "We haven't seen your *husband*! Now leave us alone, you horrible thing! Get!"

"Maybe *you* haven't seen him, but someone else in your household might have. All I'm asking for is a little time."

"I said *we*. As in *we*!" She smirked. "Maybe he's left you. Wouldn't that be something? Maybe he's found himself a good woman. A good God-fearing woman. No. Nobody here has seen your filthy friend."

"You're a liar!" David said. "And I don't know why you are lying, but I intend to find out." David looked past Sally at Michelle. "Have you seen him? Please, if you have—"

"How dare you!" Sally eeked. "Get off our porch! Go!"

She shut the door in his face. David wanted to break it down. He wanted to smash a few windows. Sally had the kind of face and demeanor that made one want to do such things. He knew it was hypocritical, but David had always found bigotry in women so much uglier than bigotry in men. Men, as rule, were unpleasant creatures. Women were supposed to be nurturing.

He stood still and collected himself. He would come back later, after everyone in the house was asleep. Something about this "family" didn't sit right with him. He knew they had something to do with Cliff's disappearance. From his short exchange with Sally, he now had that certainty.

AT THAT moment, in the basement of the Jones's old residence, just as David was walking away, Cliff found himself in a new position. He was now on his feet. His ankles and wrists were bound to the support beams in the center of the basement, the ball gag was in his mouth, and his boxer shorts were down around his ankles. Behind him, Mr. Scott had a leather belt and was laying wide red marks across Cliff's muscular ass. Cliff's ass shook with each strike. Mr. Scott smiled as he did his duty, believing his methods would work, *were* working. The television flickered the silent images of naked women before them. Newt, having come downstairs to tell Mr. Scott about David's appearance at the front door, was now seated on the steps, watching the aversion therapy at work. Every slap of leather on Cliff's ass was harder. Newt flinched each time the belt hit flesh.

"Why you hitting him so hard, sir?" Newt asked. "Has he been so bad?"

"Yes, Brother Newt," Mr. Scott answered, eyes blazing. "He most certainly has. Yes, yes."

"Poor Mr. Cliff," Newt said.

"Don't you worry about Mr. Cliff," Mr. Scott said. "I'll beat it out of him!" He swung at Cliff again and again. "I'll beat the gay away!"

Of course, if Mr. Scott had taken the time to investigate Cliff with any skill, he would have known of the ten films Cliff had done with just such a whipping scene, including *The Silence of the Gams*. He would have known that this wasn't therapy. This wasn't even torture. This was a Sunday afternoon at Cliff's house. Still, Cliff was clearly more annoyed than turned on, occasionally rolling his eyes at the proceedings. It was only when Newt said that David had been at the door that Cliff's dick lifted.

"Gay away!" Mr. Scott began to chant. "Gay away! Gay away!"

Newt joined in the chant with glee, clapping his hands as he went.

Sally soon came rushing down the stairs, nearly falling over Newt.

"Foolish child!" she chided the boy. "Move!" She rushed to the old man. "Mr. Scott!" she said, catching her breath at the sight of Cliff's rosy ass.

"What?" Mr. Scott groaned in annoyance as he lay down another smack.

"The other one, the boyfriend, was here," Sally said.

Cliff's dick hardened some more.

"The boy told me," Mr. Scott said.

"I think the boyfriend is going to be a problem."

Mr. Scott turned to look at her. "Then so shall we, Sister. There is no need to concern yourself. Everything is working out fine. We'll just need to speed up our plan is all. Nothing to it, I say." He looked back at Cliff's ass. "And this one"—he traced the curve of the raw glutes with the belt—"he'll be seeing the error of sinful ways very soon. I can tell. Yes, yes. I can tell I'm on the verge of a breakthrough. A great big explosion of godly love."

RICK had not been able to shake Michelle from his thoughts since catching her sneaking around the neighborhood the day before. He had seen her face somewhere else. He was certain of that. But where? It was like a chigger. The more he scratched at it, the more it itched.

He was at Hot Body Gym but could not concentrate on work. At this point, though, the basics of his job were done on autopilot. He racked his brain as he racked the weights until at last something was jarred from his memory.

He told his coworkers he needed to head home. There was an emergency. That wasn't a complete lie. At least not to him. It would have been terribly disappointing if he lost his train of thought, however unlikely.

Once home, he made a direct path to the kitchen computer. He was sure he'd remembered who the young woman was. He turned on the old computer, then waited impatiently for it to do its ritual song and dance. Ten minutes of loading passed, and Rick was a nervous wreck. The excitement of revelation, the annoyance of having to wait even longer for an answer, the seeming nonchalance of the lazy-ass computer—they all conspired to make him boil.

"Come on! Come on!" he shouted as he hit the side of the monitor. "Stupid head."

Well, that was apparently over the line for the kitchen PC, because it went obstinate and bluescreened. Rick looked at it, shoulders slumped. He rose to his feet and then casually knocked the entire thing onto the floor. Rick had murdered the kitchen computer.

"Stupid head," he mumbled again. He raced up to the bedroom where his trusty laptop sat like royalty on the bed. He turned the laptop on and was immediately connected to the interweb.

"I don't know why I didn't come to you first," he said.

All he had to do was type in a few key phrases—a town, a street, a tragedy—and the link to a newspaper article popped up. Success! It was the story of something that had happened not far from where he'd lived before moving to Jasper Lane. Three members of a family had been murdered—stabbed or suffocated—and the house set on fire. A fourth member, a teenage girl, was missing. There had been a search for the girl and an investigation into the killings, but there was no evidence to solve either mystery. The girl remained missing and the murders unsolved.

Beside the article there was a family photo. The girl looked amazingly similar to the young lady Michelle. There was that same unimpressed stare, though her hair in the photograph was much more nicely done than the girl he saw on Jasper Lane. They were a well-off family by all appearances.

Still looking at the photograph on the screen, Rick called Terrence. Terrence answered as if he was in the middle of something irritating and dreadfully important.

"Terrence," Rick said, "get online. I'm sending you a link."

"Yum," Terrence said. "Is it sexy men?"

"Better. I think I found out the identity of one of our new neighbors. The girl looks an awful lot like the girl in this photo I'm looking at."

"Got it," Terrence said. There was a shuffling and a tapping of keys. Terrence yelled, "Shut up, you talentless cunt" to someone and then went quiet. "Holy shit!" he said. "That's her! That's the girl!"

"I think so too."

"What should we do? Should we call the po-po?"

"No. We have no real proof it's her. And besides, she's of age now to decide where she wants to live. What if she ran away and is living here by choice? What would be the point of calling the police?"

"Oh, this is juicy! This is too terribly juicy."

Then Rick heard a bitch fight ensue as Terrence's guest, on hearing the word "juicy" and commenting that he too wanted to see what was so dee-lish, got too close for Terrence's comfort. It was broken up by Harry. Harry was sounding very annoyed with Terrence of late.

"I've got to go," Terrence said. "Bitches be trippin'. But I'm all over this bit of news, Rick. All over it."

SuburbaNights: Vignettes from Jasper Lane

WHEN Becky Ridgeworth returned home from work that day, she found that her front door was unlocked. She never forgot to lock her doors. When she was growing up on the pig farm, there had been no need to lock the house doors. They lived so far out in the country that it was rare they received an invited visitor, let alone an unwanted one. But the process had become something automatic by now. Shut door. Lock door. Such was the way of the twenty-first century. But here it was. Unlocked. She was being thieved! Pirated and thieved and invaded upon. Perhaps she should have taken that gun her daddy offered her when she moved to the Lane after all.

She quietly crept into the house and grabbed the large Silver Phallus Award from the table for protection. Becky had become quite the gay porn producer and had been showered with honors lately. The Silver Phallus wasn't as prestigious an award as the Golden Prostate, but it definitely had more girth.

She listened carefully to the house. There was a scuffling and a rummaging coming from upstairs. The chills played her like an instrument.

Quietly, like the heroine in a made-for-TV movie starring Valerie Bertinelli, she climbed the stairs. She wanted to scream for help, but that thought didn't occur to her until she was halfway up the steps. She knew she should have just run next door, but she was already in the thick of it now. Besides, she could take care of herself. She was a strong woman with backbone. She had been raised on a pig farm, dammit! Plus, she had a pair of deafening lungs and a big ol' Silver Phallus.

As she approached her bedroom door, she suddenly felt a stab of pain in her belly. She gasped and doubled over on the landing, dropping the Silver Phallus Award with a big thud. Immediately a shadow was upon her. She screamed.

"Rebecca Luanne!" her father yelled, rushing to her side. "Are you all right?"

He helped her to her feet. His callused hands always felt so gentle on her skin.

"Daddy," Becky said, the pain having passed. "What in the world are you doing here?"

"I told you I was coming. Don't think that your cell phone trick ended the conversation on my end. And it looks like I got here just in time. We're getting you to the hospital this minute. I was just in there packing you a bag." He bent over to pick up the Silver Phallus Award. "You dropped your tallywacker, baby girl."

"Daddy, I'm fine." She took the award off his hands. "I'm not going to the hospital."

"And I say yes you are, and your pappy knows best. Now let's move, else I'll have your brothers come and get you. You'll be back on the farm until this baby is born. I know you don't want *that*."

"Daddy!"

"Honey," he said, his voice sounding as gentle as his sad eyes, "it may be nothing. It probably is. But I don't want to lose you the way I lost your mom. Please. Do this for my own sanity. The thought of something happening to you keeps me up at night."

Becky knew she was going to go to the hospital now. A short vacation in a drab location. Her father rarely smiled anymore. Not since her mother had passed away from cancer ten years ago. Now it was just him and her brothers on the farm. Her brothers were sweet guys, but they were as dumb as mules.

"Oh, Daddy," Becky said with a sigh. "You manipulative old badger. Get my bag. Let's go."

"Thank you, baby girl," he said, and he kissed her on the forehead. "This will be a load off my mind." He pointed to the Silver Phallus Award. "Do you want me to pack that?"

CASSIE and Melinda made a stop for gas a few hours into their trip. They needed a rest and to stretch their legs. They had gossiped a good stretch of the way about everything from Terrence's relationship with Harry ("I don't hear wedding bells." "I hear they're splitting.") to

Cliff's sudden disappearance. Melinda ogled the Cadillac some more and made certain Cassie knew that she would most certainly be interested if Cassie ever thought of selling the car. Cassie had originally given Melinda the power of DJ as they drove, but after half an hour of nothing but adult contemporary stations, Cassie had had enough and turned to something with more of a Latin flavor. If they were going to be driving at night, she needed to stay awake.

Melinda went into the store for food and beverages. Cassie pumped the gas. It had been a while, so she had forgotten how very expensive driving the Caddy was. She put the top up so they wouldn't get too cold on the drive, and then leaned against the hood of the car to wait for Melinda.

"Cassie Bloom!"

She heard her name called loud and profane and turned to see a big white school van pulling up to the pump beside her. James Cooper-Tucker hung out the passenger-side window. He looked like a college kid on his way to a football game.

"James?" Cassie said with a smile. "What is all of this? Where is Rick?"

"Rick is back home." He got out of the car and opened the sliding door in back. "I'm helping Nips with these knuckleheads," he said.

The noisy wrestlers cheered their hellos at Cassie.

Coach Nipple came around from the driver's seat. "Hey there, Miss Bloom. What are you doing so far away from the Lane? We've been following you the whole way."

"I'm taking a drive with Melinda."

"Melinda?" The poor love-struck fool straightened up from his relaxed demeanor at once. If he had had a gut, he would have sucked it in.

"She's inside." Cassie winked and nodded toward the store. "Go say hello. I'm sure she would like that."

"I'll pump the gas," James said.

Coach Nipple went inside, taking broad steps in his well-fitting sweatpants.

"I'll keep these hooligans entertained," Cassie said. "How about it, boys?" She approached the van.

They hollered as if they were about to get a show.

"Guys," James chided, "Miss Bloom is a lady. Show some respect."

Cassie sat up front in the passenger's seat and looked back at the wrestlers with a smile. "Do we know any good songs? Any naughty limericks?"

"What's a limerick?" one of the wrestlers asked.

While Cassie was teaching the van full of horny teenagers naughty rhymes by dead poets, the coach found Melinda contemplating licorice whips in the candy aisle of the gas station's store.

"Reminds me of some good times," he said. "I have a van outside if you want to bring that whip along."

Melinda jumped and then, on seeing Coach Nipple standing there, swatted at him. "You scared me!" she said. "What are you doing here?"

"Wrestling trip. Wanna play? We're going to start adding girls to the team." His smile encouraged her own.

"No, I do not want to play," she said, walking to the next aisle, nose in the air like the popular girl in school.

"You know, the air down here is just as good for your nose."

She rolled her eyes.

"You know you wanna get dirty with me," he said.

"I do not! I don't get dirty. Now be quiet before anyone hears you talking like this." She looked around at the other patrons in the store.

"Liar. You want to tie me up. I can see it in your pretty little eyes. Diva!"

"Yes. I want to tie you up. I want to tie you up and leave you behind."

Malcolm was sliding up to whatever side of the face Melinda was ignoring him with. "What was that you said about my behind?"

Another swat and another attempt at hiding a grin. Now patrons *were* looking.

"Come on, Mel. You know you're going to have to give us another go. It's just a matter of time. We're like peanut butter and jelly."

She picked a couple of colas from the fridge for Cassie and herself. Malcolm poked her in the side, and she yelped. "Stop that!"

"Promise me a date when we get back home, Mel."

"I will not!" She walked to the register.

He poked her again. "Promise me."

She turned and wagged a finger at him even as she battled a grin. "Stop it."

He raised his eyebrows, threatening to poke her again with an itchy finger.

"Oh, all right! One date. Then it's over. Now leave me alone. I don't like you." She paid the cashier and quickly headed for the door.

"No. You don't like me," the coach said. "You *love* me." He turned back to the beleaguered cashier. "She *loves* me," he restated.

Back out in the van, Cassie was leading the boys in a blistering sample of "Mamma Mia" just as Melinda came outside. Even James was singing along, bobbing and weaving on the concrete. The coach was back at Melinda's side before she knew it. The team was allowed to complete their number before the coach interrupted.

"Thank you, Miss Bloom," Coach Nipple said.

"Thank you, Miss Bloom!" the boys cheered in unison.

"You bet," Cassie said as she slid out of the van. "Are you ready to get back on the road?" she asked Melinda.

Melinda nodded in the positive and walked with her bag of goodies to the Caddy. Cassie stared after her, then looked at the coach with a grin before heading to the Caddy herself.

"Don't forget, Mel," the coach shouted from the driver's seat of the van. "When we get back home, I'm all yours."

The boys catcalled as the van drove away, James once again waving from the passenger's seat.

"There goes a fun group of guys," Cassie said.

Melinda avoided Cassie's gaze for as long as she could but soon realized the Caddy would not move from the spot until the obvious had been addressed.

"We're going on a date," Melinda explained. "When we get back, we're going on a single date. That's all."

It was clear from her expression that Cassie loved this. "Well, it's about time."

"It's not like I had any choice. He practically accosted me in there. I mean, I could sue. I could probably get a lot of money."

"And that turned you on? His accosting of you?"

"What? No." Melinda grinned, staring out her window. "Absolutely not."

UNDER cover of darkness, David donned dark clothing and a black knitted cap. In what was becoming standard practice for the residents of Jasper Lane, he snuck through other people's backyards. He had thought of asking Terrence to help him, but that would have only ended in disaster. Terrence would have certainly gotten them caught. Life was a cabaret to Terrence. A fucking tacky cabaret. And what was a cabaret without music? David thought this was something he needed to do alone.

From behind a tree, David watched the Jones's old place for signs of life or, that being unlikely, at least signs of movement. He wondered how long it would take everyone to stop calling the house "the Jones's old place." The truth was, that was all it could be called at the moment. Other than Mr. Scott, the rest of this "family" had no surname. They were just the Crazies. The nickname was not particularly clever, but then, neither were they.

The lights in the house were still on, and it was late. Not knowing the family, David wasn't sure what this signified. Sometimes people left their lights on all night, even when they slept. He could see no human forms through the thick closed curtains. He could hear no voices, television, or movement.

He came closer to the house, looking into windows but seeing nothing. Damn curtains. The basement windows were locked tight and covered. He pushed on the glass, but there was no give. They weren't going to budge short of him breaking them, and they were too small for David to fit through anyway.

The exterior basement door was padlocked on the outside. This was an easier challenge. Having learned to pick locks from James, David was finally able to put the skill to the test here. He set to work, and moments later, with one satisfying click, the lock came off. He carefully opened the door. The steps were cluttered with trash left behind by Steve and Sandy. A croquet set. Old Christmas decorations. A broken fan. David climbed over them to the large plywood board covering the doorway. Luckily, it wasn't adhered to the wall, and with some exertion, he was finally able to push his way into the basement. He could only hope that he wasn't being too loud.

At first he wasn't sure what he was seeing. It was mostly dark, and his eyes didn't adjust immediately. Then a light flickered. There was a television, and it was loud. And in front of it….

David nearly yelled: *Cliff!*

There Cliff was, bound and naked on a worn-out mattress. Cliff's eyes were wide with joy at seeing his hubby, though he could say nothing with the ball gag still in his mouth. David rushed over to him. It was as if they hadn't seen each other in months.

"What the hell is this?" David said, taking the ball gag away and throwing it across the room.

They kissed hungrily while Cliff whispered.

"This family," he said, "they're fucking nuts! They're not even a real family. Just some religious cult trying to turn me straight."

"By tying you naked to a mattress?" David worked at the binding and chains on Cliff's wrists.

"And that." Cliff nodded to the vagina show. "This guy thinks he's some kind of aversion therapy genius."

"What an asshole. We're going to get you out of here, babe, and then we'll have these assholes arrested."

"Baby! I'm so happy to see you. They were planning to come for you next. Davey, I've known some real twisted folk in my life, but Mr. Scott takes the cake. We gotta hurry."

But no sooner had Cliff spoken than David collapsed in a heap onto his chest.

"You'll not interfere with the Lord's glorious plans." Mr. Scott stood over them, having knocked David out with the butt of a gun. "Clearly, the Lord our God has deigned to make it easier on us, brothers and sisters, by having this new sinner come to us of his own accord."

"Amen." Sally and Newt echoed Mr. Scott's sentiment from somewhere behind him. Michelle was silent as she retrieved the ball gag and gave it to Mr. Scott.

Before this, Cliff had been annoyed. Now he was furious. As Mr. Scott bent down to put the ball gag back in his mouth, Cliff caught the old man's finger in his mouth and bit down on it hard. Blood gushed out, and the old man howled and tripped backwards. Cliff was able to spit the finger back out before he too was knocked unconscious by the butt of a gun.

The Chapter in Which Terrence Is Mistaken for a TV Star

MICHELLE made short work of poor Newt.

It happened the next morning. Having fastened the unconscious David to a mattress similar in quality to the one Cliff lay on, Mr. Scott told his two youngest followers to seal the exterior basement entrance up so that no other degenerates could find their way in. The plywood board was then to be fixed to the wall with a crude cement, and, from the outside, the step well was to be filled in with large rectangular blocks that Sally had stolen from a nearby construction site—that of a new movie theater, so she didn't feel bad about it. Michelle handed the large blocks down to Newt, one by one, and Newt fixed them good and tight. Newt seemed to think his job of supreme importance and so adjusted the bricks this way and that as if he were putting together a window display at a fancy department store. This meticulous attention to detail would be maddening to some. Every brick took a good five minutes to lay, sometimes longer.

Maddening.

As Newt was laying the bricks, he spoke on and on about how lucky they were to know the truth of God. About how wonderful Mr. Scott was to take them under his wing. About how Michelle could never appreciate any of this fully because, as Sally had said on numerous occasions before, "You're nothing but a deaf mute."

And so some might say that Michelle had every right to start pitching the bricks at Newt's head. Some might say that an early-

93

morning annoyance justified an early-morning homicide. Some might say that.

Michelle wouldn't have cared one way or the other what some might say, though, and she couldn't be fazed by the blood either. Its redness no longer shocked her. She simply walled Newt up with the remaining bricks and padlocked the cellar door behind her.

TERRENCE wanted to take the new vase he had just recently purchased for the hall bureau and smash it against the wall like an old-school Hollywood pro. How dare Harry side with those inbred religious fiends! How dare Harry not see that the cross in their front yard looked ten times better in pink!

That was what the argument was about—the painting of the cross. Well, maybe not *about* so much as what the argument masqueraded as being about. Beneath that mask both Terrence and Harry knew there were other issues kicking at them, but this was as good a point as any to take up fighting over.

They had been enjoying a moment of sublime snuggling when Harry—that lumberjack of a boyfriend whom Terrence had met at the father/son outing with Chris—brought the matter up.

"Did you see what someone did to the cross on your street?" he asked. "Someone painted it pink."

Terrence, neither thinking before he spoke nor speaking with any great thought, said, while resting his head on Harry's chest, "That was me and the Girls."

Harry sat up in the bed immediately. "What?"

"Yep. We did that." He was proud of the job, but his look of pride changed to confusion when he saw the shocked expression on Harry's face.

"Why would you do that?"

"They're jerks who needed a little color in their lives. They asked for it. We brought it."

"It's the cross, Terry!"

Harry got up and started pulling on his clothes.

"So? It doesn't mean anything to me."

"It means something to me! Doesn't that count?"

"Why are you getting so upset? It's a piece of wood. An idol, right? Come back to bed." Terrence patted the mattress playfully. "Let me paint *your* idol."

Harry was dumbfounded. "You really don't care, do you? You don't give a shit about what's important to me."

He left the room half-dressed. Terrence jumped up from the bed and followed him.

"Why do you hate Christians so much, Terry?"

"I don't hate all of them," Terrence said. "Just some of them. Those crazy bastards down the street are different from you and Chris."

"How?" Harry asked on the stairs as he turned around to face Terrence.

"Duh. I don't hate you."

"But you do feel superior to us. Admit it."

"What's that got to do with anything? I feel superior to everyone."

"Wrong answer." Harry marched down the steps, pulling his T-shirt over his head.

"Where are you going?" Terrence asked.

"Home. Where I'm loved and not just tolerated. I'll call you later. Maybe." He slammed the door behind him.

"You are being such a drama queen!" Terrence screamed after him.

He stood at a loss for any more coherent words, yet wanting to scream. "What the fuck was that?" he wondered.

Instead of throwing an expensive vase, he picked up the pillows from the sofa and launched them across the room.

Harry had gotten him thinking, though. Terrence found his cell phone and dialed Chris's number. There was no answer, which usually meant Chris was in class. Chris never avoided calls. When his voice mail picked up, Terrence cleared his throat.

"Hey, Chris," he said. "It's Terrence... your dad... daddy... father... whatever. Listen, um, how would you like to take me to one of those cathedral places or churches? I would like to, um, learn about God, I guess. I hear there are wafers and wine, so it can't be all bad, right? I like wafers and wine. *Especially* wine. Could be a party. Anyway, just get back to me. Talk later. Love you!"

He felt better. Like he was making an effort. The truth was, though, he knew he wouldn't feel totally normal again until he got everything hammered out with Harry. How dare he march out the door in a huff! That was Terrence's part! Everybody seemed to be overreacting lately but him.

He pulled on a hoodie and flip-flops and chugged across the street to tell David about the spat he had just endured. Talking with David always made Terrence feel better, even if David never had any advice to give. But then, Terrence was never really looking for advice, just an audience. Terrence rarely took advice.

The moment he walked into David' house, he sensed it was empty. Still, he called out as he took a tour of the place. There was no answer. The bed was unmade, the kitchen light was on, the car was in the garage, but there was no one home. Terrence scratched his head in confusion.

He tried calling David's cell. The ringtone—an infectious pop song that would be outdated in three minutes—went off immediately in the den, where David had apparently left it. *What and where the hell?*

Then Terrence remembered what Rick had told him about the murdered family and the missing girl—the same missing girl who now lived on Jasper Lane. As Terrence was a raging conspiracy nut, the idea that David, and Cliff too, had been kidnapped by the people who had kidnapped that girl made perfect sense to Terrence. And now she had been brainwashed to join them and kidnap innocent people all over the city, forcing them to work in diamond mines or Chick-fil-As.

Terrence covered his mouth as if he had just had an epiphany. The kidnappers might be in the house this very moment watching him, waiting to come out of the closet and attack him. He would be outnumbered.

Oh, poor David and Cliff!

Terrence backed out of the house, fumbling to find the door knob while keeping an eye on his surroundings. Finally outside, he began racing back across the street as fast as his flip-flops would allow. Some crazy bitches had stolen his best friends, and he had a good idea of just which crazy bitches these crazy bitches were.

"WE'RE lost," Melinda stated. "There is no denying it."

She and Cassie sat on the hood of the Cadillac on a rural road, watching a dead cornfield being touched by the morning sun. They both wore jackets and confused expressions.

"Yes, dear," Cassie said. "We've been lost for the past hour and a half. I was just driving around hoping to come across some sign. We should be close to that camp by now. If only there was a sign."

"From God?"

"Or the highway system. Either would do. I'm not stingy with my prayers."

"I offered to drive."

"I appreciate that. I should have taken you up on your offer. The sleepier I get, the worse is my sense of direction. I need one of those GPS gadgets, but having someone barking commands at me while I drive would be distracting."

"I don't like the woman's voice on those things. She's a know-it-all."

"That would be the point, wouldn't it?"

They had stopped twice for coffee during the night, but neither of the stops was very long. Now, the coffees they had purchased were cold and bland, and they hadn't had a real meal since leaving Jasper Lane.

A flock of geese flew overhead in a big V.

Cassie sighed. "I wish I knew where Jason was. I wish he would just call me."

There was a note in her voice that Melinda recognized as desperation. She put an arm around Cassie. "We'll find him."

"I guess we should get going," Cassie said, wiping a tear from her cheek. "There has to be a town up ahead. Maybe a gas station where we could find some directions. You can't go too far in America without running right into somewhere else."

"Maybe we could get directions to a nice hotel. You need to sleep, and I need a shower."

"I don't think I could sleep."

"You're going to try."

Cassie looked at Melinda with a raised eyebrow. "Are you in control now?"

"I am. I'm the boss of you, at least until you get a clearer head. I don't want to die in a car wreck because of your sleep deprivation." She held out her hand. "Now, give me the keys."

"They're in the ignition." Cassie got to her feet, and Melinda followed.

"Let's get out of here," Melinda said as the ladies got back into the Caddy. "These type of back road spots are rife with serial murderers and violent teenagers. I've seen movies about it." She turned the ignition. "I've never met a murderer, and I don't intend to start now."

Cassie held her tongue. Again.

COBY climbed down from his mounted position on Seth and rested, satisfied, on yet another motel bed at the same cheap-ass motel. The sheets were a twisted mess. The floor was littered with clothes and condom wrappings. The air smelled like sweaty man. They had been at it all night.

"Sweet Lord," Coby said breathlessly. "I never thought I'd ever top a hairy rugby player. That was something else!"

Seth winked. "I owed it to you after the way I've been treating your poor ass lately."

"Well, I appreciate it. Words can't tell you how much I do."

"Honestly, Coby," Seth said, giving a sideways look of playful suspicion, "I never thought I'd ever enjoy fucking a skinny-ass tweaker, but you have proven me wrong." He took a cigarette from his nearby gym bag and sat up in bed.

"You smoke?" Coby asked.

"No. I used to. I kicked it. I just like the feel of a cigarette between my lips after good sex." He stuck the cigarette between his lips, a bad boy affectation in a sleazy motel room. "Call it an oral fixation."

"That *was* good sex."

"That was great sex."

They sat in silence for a moment, soaking in the euphoric post-sex atmosphere. Coby stretched, arms above his head and hands curled into bony fists. Seth rubbed Coby's stomach and glided his fingers over Coby's rib cage.

"You either need to eat more or use less. You are skin and bones, boy. If we keep having sex as rough as we do, I'm afraid I'll break you at some point."

Coby shrugged.

"How well do you know Rick?" Seth asked.

"Well enough." Coby seemed a little put out by the inquiry. "I was the one who caused him to lose the eye. I'm the bad guy in his story."

Seth looked at him, expecting more of the tale.

"It was an accident. Let's just say something that was meant for me got him instead. I piss people off. A lot of people. I don't mean to.

99

But people in my line of work tend to have long memories and short fuses."

"Christ almighty. You need a new line of work."

"For a while I tried to win Rick back. I even tried to go legit. Got a real job. I was working on a way to break him and James up too. But I'm no good at being devious unless it's unintentional. And then it usually just bites me in the ass."

"I was trying to do the same," Seth said. "Breaking James and Rick up, I mean. Maybe we should try to do it as a team."

"But then, who would get Rick if we were successful? I'm right in thinking you had a wee crush on Rick as well, right?"

"Yeah. Point taken."

Coby rose for the shower. Seth watched him, something appreciative in his stare. He folded his arms across his thick chest, deep in thought, the cigarette hanging loose on his bottom lip.

"Skinny little tweaker," Seth chuckled.

Coby said nothing as he disappeared into the bathroom and turned on the water.

Only a second later, there came a shrill shriek. Seth jumped up just as Coby came stumbling out of the bathroom.

"What the fuck?" Seth yelled. "Was the water too cold?"

Coby shook his head and, with saucer eyes, pointed at the floor in front of the bathtub. "Look at the size of that motherfucking spider!"

Seth rolled his eyes, ready to condescend, but then his mouth dropped open.

Both naked men shivered as they beheld a truly Shelobian arachnid, black as night and looking pissed.

"Is somebody feeding that thing small children?" Coby said.

"Kill it," Seth said, standing just a little behind Coby.

"*You* kill it. I'd be a snack for something like that."

Seth found an outdated magazine on the bureau and rolled it up, approaching with some trepidation the giant spider. Instead of shrinking away as he approached, however, the vicious thing rushed him and stood on hind legs, clearly with evil intent. Seth screamed just as shrilly as Coby had done and rushed into Coby's arms.

"Did you see that? I mean, did you *see* that?" Seth yelled.

The spider clambered forward again.

"Don't let it get out!" Coby screamed.

Seth slammed the bathroom door closed. Both of them ran for the bed and jumped on it as if the room were crawling with the critters. After a moment of shivering and making damn well certain that was the only spider in their vicinity, they calmed down. Then they began to smile. Then they began to laugh. Then they kissed.

Then, very quickly, they dressed and left.

DAVID woke fastened hard to a filthy used mattress. He shook off his daze as he tried to comprehend his situation and surroundings. He was naked but for his boxer briefs, and gagged with a washcloth. He recognized the dark basement as that of Steve and Sandy's. He and Cliff had helped them clean it once. What the hell was going on?

Across the room, Cliff's smiling eyes reassured him. David's face was flooded yet again with relief. Cliff was alive. That was all he could ask for, captivity be damned.

Cliff winked and made his penis jump up to say hello. David laughed through the gag in his mouth. At least they were together.

The television had been turned to face David now. Cliff was spared any more of the Vagina Videologues, at least for the time being. Not that either David or Cliff were paying much attention to the women on the television. The TV gave off an ample supply of light, so they had one another for entertainment. Even when Mr. Scott came down (hand firmly bandaged from Cliff's attack) and began angrily babbling on about his mission, about how he was sent by God to direct every single person on Jasper Lane to the narrow pathway leading to salvation, even then Cliff and David only had eyes for each other.

If David and Cliff were paying attention very closely to anything Mr. Scott was saying, they might have noticed the heightened stress in his voice when he said, "We've lost one. Brother Newt. Yes, our boy Brother Newt has apparently turned his back on the faith and disappeared into this filthy world."

They would have heard Mr. Scott blame them for this abandonment.

"As queer as the two of you," Mr. Scott said, "I could tell that boy was. Yes, yes. The temptation was too strong for Brother Newt. I know it. I mean, I've seen it. I mean, I *saw* it. In him. Temptation, that is…."

Mr. Scott might just as well have not been there at all, though. He surely sensed this, for he stopped in his rant and looked from one of them to the other.

"You will hear me," he warned. "You *will*. I swear it."

He held his bandaged hand (an infection had set in, but he refused the extravagance of modern medicine), and then he went upstairs.

"Gay away!" he shouted before he shut the door and latched it.

At last, they were alone again. Yet David had been stoking Cliff's fire the entire time Mr. Scott had been ranting. A certain wink or lift of the eyebrow and they both knew what the other was thinking. And poor Cliff was such a sexual creature, such a nymphomaniac, that the few days without David's touch had built in him an energy ready to explode. His balls ached. All he needed was a look from David, and that was exactly what he was getting now. In spades.

One marvelous fact about Cliff, and one that David found endlessly entertaining, was the big guy's ability to cum without putting hand to groin. Turn him on and he would get off all by himself. This talent had been put to use in a number of Cliff's films. And on this day, from across the basement, David had given his humpy hubby a hand job by eye hint. Cliff's dick rose and strained as if being licked and teased, reaching out for David until it pointed painfully erect, sculptural in its vascularity. Cliff's balls churned, full of testosterone that needed to be discharged. Cliff knew what he had to do. He moved his abdomen in and out, clenching and releasing muscles for a few frenzied moments, and then *KABOOM!*

Good to see you, baby! I've missed you so much.

MELINDA and Cassie flopped down exhausted onto their beds. They had found a small hotel for the night, someplace nice but not too expensive. As they paid for their room, they asked for directions to the camp. They planned to head out once they had had a light rest and had both showered. Of the two of them lying there now, Cassie was the worse for the wear.

"Don't let me sleep too long," Cassie said in a slow sleepy voice. "Two hours at the most, darling. We must get back on the road."

"Are you a difficult person to wake up?" Melinda was staring up at the elegant crown molding on the ceiling.

"I'm a light sleeper, my dear. I wake up at the sound of leaves on the roof. You'll have no problem. Just have a Bloody Mary waiting for me."

"I'll try and be quiet." Melinda rubbed her eyes, sitting up and looking toward the shower. "The things our families get us into." She shook her head. "Mothers and their children. I sometimes think that if Patrick had been a girl, my life would have been much easier. Do you ever think like that, Cassie?"

"I've never really thought about it. But I suppose it's possible if Jason had been Janice, things might not have turned out as... adventurous."

"Girls are more obedient, I think."

Cassie smiled, her eyes still closed. "Are they?"

"Maybe that's the wrong word. What I mean is, girls are more cautious. Yes. That's it. They seem to want to please their parents more. At least, I did. I can't say Nanna was ever very pleased with anything I did, though."

"I did too."

Melinda stared at her. "Really? You?"

"Absolutely. I loved my parents very much. They were good parents. And I was a very controlled young lady. High quality, I had been called by my parents' friends. I was proud of that fact. It was only in college that my wild streak kicked in, that the woman you know now began to show. Why, before that I bet I could have given you a run for your Goody Two-shoes, Melinda Gold." Cassie sighed. "But thinking about it, I can't imagine not having Jason. I can't imagine raising a girl. I wouldn't trade him for the world. He has such character, such... star quality. And let's not forget that your Patrick is a prince among young men. You should be proud of him."

"I am. I really am. I miss him awfully sometimes."

"By the way," Cassie said, her voice beginning to fade and drift, "Patrick sent me something the other day...."

"Did he? He's always thinking of others. He's always sending gifts or cards or giving me a phone call right when I need to hear from him most. He even sent me a batch of cookies last month. I don't think he made them, though. They were awful. But he sent them, and that's half as good. And they were boxed very nicely too."

"He is a very kind young man. But what he sent me...." Fading, fading. "You need to see...."

"And did I tell you what he sent me *last* week?" Melinda said this competitively. "A rose. A single rose. It was so lovely, and it came in this hand-blown vase. I wonder if he personally blew it? Does he know how to blow, do you think? Can Patrick blow things?"

Cassie chuckled, even in her sleep.

"What was it he sent you?" Melinda asked.

But, of course, by this point Cassie was fast asleep.

Melinda quietly rose from her bed and gathered her things for a shower. Cassie didn't stir. As she hadn't slept in well over a day, Melinda was certain it would take a bit more noise than usual to wake her. She wasn't certain about having a Bloody Mary waiting for her friend when she awoke, however. Not if they were going to get going first thing.

"*GAY Man!*" Mr. Ridgeworth shouted as he squinted at Terrence over Becky's legs. Becky lay in a hospital bed that looked about as comfortable as Terrence felt. Mr. Ridgeworth had the same facial expression for Terrence every time they met: that of utter confusion. Terrence sat cross-legged in his chair, staring at Mr. Ridgeworth and clearly annoyed. He drummed his fingers along his pant leg.

"It's *Gay Man Shopper*, right? That's the show you were on. The one about all those gay boys shopping for the straight ones."

"Daddy," Becky said, shaking her head in embarrassment, "Terrence has never been on TV. You ask him this every time you see him."

"I know it was one of those trendy shows," her father said, ignoring her. "My boys could use some help in their wardrobes, let me tell you. Maybe you could come on down to the pig farm with me."

"Well, that would be an adventure," Terrence said.

"Which show was it?" Mr. Ridgeworth continued with his interrogation. "No. Never mind. Don't tell me. I'll figure it out. Was it a home renovation program? A dating game?"

"Daddy!"

He hushed, but he still watched Terrence as if he were a Picasso painting with a tit on the forehead. The old man rubbed his chin in contemplation.

"What has the doctor said?" Terrence asked, turning his attention to Becky.

"They're running more tests," Becky replied. "They know it's just gas, though. *I* know it's just gas. Even *Daddy* knows it's just gas, but—"

"Better safe than sorry, baby girl," Mr. Ridgeworth cut in. "Was it one of those medical reality programs? Like *House*?"

"That's not a reality show, Daddy."

"The hell it ain't."

105

"Anyway," Becky continued, "I'm going to stay here until Daddy is satisfied that there is nothing life-threatening going on. The insurance won't cover it, but he will. All that pig farming has made my daddy a rich man."

"The baby is fine?" Terrence asked.

"The baby is more than fine. The little monster is doing somersaults inside of me."

"Like a cheerleader! Like me!"

"Are you on one of those homosexual sports teams?" Mr. Ridgeworth inquired. "They're popping up all over the place now. You can't turn on the television without a pro going mo. Have I seen you play on the TV?"

"'Fraid not."

"That's disappointing," Mr. Ridgeworth said. "That would have been an interesting story to tell over Thanksgiving dinner this year."

"How is the cheerleading practice coming along?" Becky asked.

"We're going to knock everyone's jocks off, Becks!" Terrence said. "There's been a bit of fighting, of course. A little hair-pulling. And Breckon Hardy, aka Liza, has quit three different times. But all in all it's been a hoot! I can't wait to show James how good we are."

"And there's still no word on where Cliff might be?"

"No." Terrence leaned forward, a sign of more urgent news to tell. "And now, David has flat-out vanished as well. I went over to his house before I came here to offer my support and to tell him about the argument Harry and I had this morning, but he was nowhere to be found. Nowhere. The door was unlocked and his car was there, but *he* was not. It's just like what happened to Cliff."

"Oh, no. What do you think is going on?"

"Nefarious deeds, is what. And I think I know just who is behind them. The Addams Family."

"The who?" Mr. Ridgeworth yelled. "Speak up! I can't follow you through all your fancy talk."

Terrence cupped his hands around his mouth and shouted across the bed. "The weird religious nuts who moved into Steve and Sandy's old place."

"Why do you think they had anything to do with it?" asked Becky.

"Because David told me he was headed over there last night, and now... *poof!* The poof has poofed. And Rick showed me a web article about a missing girl, and she looked just like the younger lady in that... *family.*"

Becky shook her head, wide-eyed and wondering. "We need to get to the bottom of this, Terrence. What if our friends are in real trouble?"

"I plan to, sweetie. Don't you worry. I'm going to head over to the Crazies' myself."

"Terrence! Be careful. When?"

"Maybe tomorrow." He looked blazingly uncertain. "If I'm going to face them all alone, I'll need to summon my courage. That will take some doing. I'm talking a night of watching fierce drag queen films."

Becky shook her fists in excitement. "Oh! I wish I could come along! You're going to be just like a Charlie's Angel."

"Mr. Ridgeworth," Terrence said, trying to play nice, "can Becky—"

"No." Then: "It's gotta be *Gay Man Shopper!*"

"For God's sake, Daddy! You've already said that one."

IT WAS perhaps Mr. Ridgeworth's talk of reality programs that caused Becky to have such a fitful sleep that night. There were no drugs being pumped into her system, so there was no other explanation for it.

Becky dreamed she was in the hospital, but her room was bright and warmly lit. It seemed almost to be a resort. The fragrances of unnamed flowers scented the air, and Becky, free of the bed, danced about the room with ease. She had white ribbons in her hair, and she sang along to The Mamas & The Papas. She dreamed her belly was bigger, yet she felt no discomfort at all. Her father was not there to tell her to stop dancing, and the nursing staff was an audience of familiar gay porn stars, each of them naked but for a stethoscope about his neck. They were all at full attention and applauded wildly as she danced. That part of the dream was lovely.

Then in walked Melinda. She was a sight to see. She was dressed so lazily, in gray sweats and tennis shoes, that it took a moment for Becky to recognize her. There was not a hint of makeup, and her hair was held back in a sloppy rushed ponytail. She held a look of such grumpiness as she puffed on a long unashed cigarette that Becky wondered aloud if Nanna Hench wasn't Melinda's real mother after all. Melinda did not reply to this. She didn't even feign insult.

Suddenly, Becky felt a sharp pain and gasped. She held her big belly and ran to the restroom.

"You okay in there?" Melinda called in a tired voice from the other side of the door.

Becky sat on the toilet, a bit annoyed by the question. The time one spent on the toilet in the restroom was private time. Sacred alone time. One should not be quizzed on how they were doing while one was trying to take a piss.

"I'm fine," Becky answered as politely as she could.

But she wasn't. Not in this dream. She spasmed, letting out a quick cry, and then felt a sudden great relief. Then, to her surprise, she heard the crying.

"What the hell is *that*?" Melinda yelled as she pushed open the restroom door, cigarette still in hand. The male porn nurses and doctors looked in over Melinda's shoulder. Their faces had gone from adoring to complete disgust. There were even a couple of audible "icky-poos."

Becky stood and looked into the toilet. There was a baby! A baby was in the toilet, looking up at her with large baby doll eyes. And it was a *big* baby.

"Holy shit!" Melinda cried, coughing through the cigarette smoke that surrounded her like fog. "You just pooped a baby!"

Of course, this was when Becky woke the hell up. Her father still rested undisturbed in the chair beside her bed. The mounted corner television was mute above her. She calmed her breathing, relieved there was no Toilet Baby to look after. Yet.

She felt her belly. Still the right size. Definitely still filled with baby.

Then she relaxed.

"Goddamn reality TV!" she cursed.

JAMES rested on his hotel bed after an interesting day with Coach Nipple and the wrestling team. He talked on his cell with Rick. Their conversation went as follows... more or less:

"Hey, baby," he said. "How was your day? Did you survive without me? Are you a blubbering mess yet?"

Rick chuckled. "I got by somehow. What you up to?"

"Just chillin' here on my bed."

"How's the hotel?"

"It's nice. I was surprised I got my own room. I thought I'd have to share."

"I bet that's a relief. Now you don't have to see a naked Coach Nipple emerge from the shower all shiny and new."

"Yeah. Who would want to see that?"

"Who on earth?"

"No one. That's who."

"Yeah. Because he's not at all attractive."

"Not at all. Not at all."

"How do you like being an assistant to that vilely unattractive man?"

"I like it a lot. It's a bit of work dealing with teenage boys, though. I forgot how much of a handful they can be. If it ain't one thing, it's another. Were you ever one of those? A teenage boy?"

"I don't think so. I believe I just appeared one afternoon in my bedroom fully formed. Well, almost. I had trouble with an eye. But who doesn't, right?"

"Right. I had trouble with sexiness. I was given too much of it. What a nuisance."

"Indeed."

"Anyway, there was a big ruckus after the match today. Whoa, doggies. It was quite the scene, but I think I handled it well."

"Do tell, handsome man."

"I shall. I was getting ready for dinner—we ate at an all-you-can-eat place across the street—and I heard some shouting in the room next door. By the way, I'm right next door to a couple of the guys on the team. That's kind of important to my story."

"Good to know."

"I was very hungry and didn't want to spend any time corralling teenagers whilst I could be eating, so I went next door to see, or have explained to me, all the hullabaloo—"

"Nice word choice."

"Thank you. All the guys on the team were packed into this one room. Apparently, they had heard the ruckus as well. The room was an absolute disaster area, but they *are* teenage boys. One of their number—we'll call him Ted—"

"What's his real name?"

"Ted. Anyway, Ted was pissed because one of the other guys—a certain Brad—had insulted him. You see, apparently Brad needed some deodorant and while searching through Ted's bag came across some porn of the penis-on-penis kind."

"Oh my."

"Yes. Indeedly so. Right off the bat I thought Brad had said something anti-gay. You know, one of those ugly words mediocre people use when describing the beautiful people we are."

"I am familiar with a few, yes."

"But that wasn't so."

"No?"

"No. In fact, Brad had told him, 'Hey, man. It gets better.'"

"Well, that was nice."

"It was. At least *I* thought it was. But Ted said he hated that YouTube bullshit. He said to Brad, 'What the hell would you know about it?'"

"He has a point."

"Maybe. But *my* point is that none of the guys gave a shit that Ted was a gay. Not one of them."

"Times have changed."

"I pulled Ted away and asked him why *he* cared if they didn't. He told me he hated being singled out. Now all the guys would see him as 'the gay one'. He couldn't even get an erection—which often happens during wrestling matches without the surging of any real sexual interest—without the other guys now wondering if maybe he was into them."

"What did you do to quell this situation, dear husband?"

"I told him about my rugby team, The Sacred Band of Thebes. That we were all gay—except for that one guy—and he should show up and play with us sometime. He was all about it. His face lit up."

"How sweet! That was very fatherly of you. You're a bit like a father figure."

"That's what he said! He said, 'Would you adopt me?' I think he was joking, but it felt nice. Real nice."

"Maybe we should look into that?"

"Into what? Adopting him? I think he has parents, baby."

"Not him specifically. But having a baby might be something to think about. I can hear you smiling. You like the idea, don't you?"

"I do. That's definitely something to consider for the next chapter of our lives."

"Chapter? Honey, that'll be a whole new book."

111

"Anything happening on the Lane? What's Terrence gotten himself into?"

"We might have a kidnappee living amongst us, and Terrence thinks she has something to do with David and Cliff's disappearances."

"Wait. David's gone now too?"

"Uh-huh. We're all a bit concerned. Rick called the police, but they didn't do much. They came over, looked around, complimented the decorations, then left."

"Well, don't you go missing too."

"I'll stick around. At least until you get home."

"Good. Because when I get home, I'm gonna be sowing my seed in your fertile fields. We're gonna have us a child."

"Wait. What? Where exactly do babies come from?"

THE basement door opened. David and Cliff's grunts and moans to each other, their secret basement language, ceased altogether. David was in the midst of explaining to Cliff, via something that sounded like primitive man in a dark cave, what he was seeing on the television— "mmmm-mmmhmm" (translation: "big vagina")—when Sally turned on the light and made her way down the steps.

"I've got cookies!" she said more cheerfully than either of them had ever heard her speak. She held a tall plate of chocolate chip cookies. Both of the hungry men's stomachs growled. The smell was intoxicating.

"They're for you," she said to Cliff. "Because you've been such a good boy today."

She turned to look at David with a flat expression. "People who break into other people's homes and try to take their things don't get cookies," she said.

David mumbled a definite sarcastic question. Translation: *"Their things? Bitch."*

Sally lowered herself onto the ratty mattress beside Cliff. "You be a good boy and let me take this gag off. No biting, please."

She looked for a place to put the plate of cookies before at last deciding on Cliff's firm tummy.

But then! Oh, the shock!

"What is *this*?" she yelled, rising to her feet. (She wore a knock-off brand of high-tops made of denim.)

Cliff's belly was painted with a white gooey substance. And there was way more than just one helping of it too. It was also apparent that some of it was freshly spilled. Sally wiped the goo she had gotten on her fingers onto her clothes.

"What...? How?"

Cliff's penis came to life and spit at Sally indignantly.

Sally's jaw remained dropped for a bit before she recovered herself, spilling some of the cookies to the floor. She quickly bent to snatch them back up, then struggled to look Cliff in the face. He was grinning at her, even with the ball gag in his mouth.

"You naughty boy!" she said. "You dirty, naughty, rude boy! How?"

She turned her gaze on David accusingly. "This is your doing! You penis poacher! You're some sort of witch, aren't you? Evil!"

She was at a loss as to what to do. Finally, she bent down and gave Cliff's dick a solid whack on its head. He and it both jumped.

"Naughty!" she cried. "You'll get none of my cookies! Either of you!"

Sally fled the room, crying, with her cookies as Cliff and David laughed beneath their gags.

"Mmmmmm!" Cliff said between his muted guffaws. Translation: "She smacked my wiener!"

"Mmmmmm!" David agreed.

The Chapter in Which Vera Tells of Terrence's Encounter With a Fucking Machine

CASSIE and Melinda had gotten up at the crack of dawn to get back on the road. Melinda had tried to wake Cassie a number of times but was met with threats and lazy shoves. This, she learned, was where the Bloody Mary would be useful. Melinda raided the minifridge and put together the drink, after which she tried waking Cassie once more. This time she was successful.

"Do you think you may have a drinking problem?" Melinda cautiously asked.

"Don't be silly," Cassie said, sipping her drink. "Of course I do. This is very good, by the way."

Their ambition was not rewarded, however, as the old Cadillac refused to start. Having risen so very early, they had to wait until the town itself—a little place annoyingly called Little Place—woke up before they could even get the car towed to a mechanic.

Cassie dealt with this irritation as she always did with such things: with a stoic grace. Melinda openly admired this as they stood in the lobby area of the first auto repair shop that opened. Mechanical things buzzed and hammered and rang out around them. The place naturally smelled of grease and boredom.

"I don't know how you're doing it," Melinda said. "I would be so... ruffled. I would have lost it hours ago."

"I can't get ruffled anymore. I've lost all my feathers, my dear. Every single one."

They stood at a window, watching the Caddy being inspected by strapping farm boys in snug blue overalls. The owner of the shop, Mr. Hardcastle—a man with world-weary eyes and a studied expression—came into the lobby and told them he could get the Caddy fixed by the weekend.

"I can't say as fixing it will keep it going much longer, though," said Mr. Hardcastle. "I don't know how much more life that old car has in it. It looks good on the outside, but the inside is a mess."

"But that won't do," Cassie said. "We need to get back on the road as soon as possible. We can't wait until this weekend."

"Her son," Melinda interjected. "We have to find her son. We think he might be in a great deal of trouble."

There was a moment, a moment even Melinda noticed, when Cassie locked eyes with Mr. Hardcastle and something passed between them.

"If you could do something to help me out, Mr. Hardcastle," Cassie said.

"Reggie," he corrected her.

"If you could do anything at all, Reggie, I would pay extra."

"No need," Reggie said. "Come by tomorrow morning. It'll be done then. I'll work on it myself. That's as soon as I can do it."

Melinda watched as Cassie seemed to age backward before her eyes. Cassie's eyes sparkled when she said, "Thank you, Reggie."

And so Cassie and Melinda had a day to wait in Little Place. The ladies found a diner near their hotel and had a late breakfast. Cassie sat staring out the window for a while, hardly touching the food that the little twink waiter brought to her. ("What can I get you fabulous ladies?" he had exclaimed upon seeing them.)

"What a cute young waiter!" Melinda said after he had given them a big grin and left their table with an extravagant bow. "He reminds me of Patrick. But then, somehow every young man around that age reminds me of Patrick."

Cassie gave the boy a studious look and smiled. "We'll leave him a big tip. The poor thing can't have too many romantic prospects in a town like this."

"Such a cutie!" Melinda repeated.

Cassie stirred her coffee. "So, what are your plans with the coach when we get back to Jasper Lane?"

"I promised him a date, so we'll go on a date."

"And?"

"No conjunction required. And *nothing*. I don't have a place for him in my life. Not at the moment."

"Melinda, darling, he's the best thing to come along for you in a very long time. When was the last time you had a relationship as exciting as what you had with Coach Nipple? Even his name is exciting. Nipple. How wonderful!"

Melinda didn't need to think very hard on that. She had never been in a relationship outside of the one she'd had with Patrick's father. Malcolm had been the first time she had truly enjoyed herself with a man. But....

"Well, what about you, Miss Cassie Bloom? Where's the romance in your life?"

"What about me? Good question. I haven't been on a real date in years. I've messed around with a few men on whims and hookups, but never anything that would amount to much."

"It's not like the world is filled with eligible men our...."

"Age. Yes. That's true. It seems at the age of forty men hit a midlife crisis that lasts until they can no longer fuck."

"There has got to be someone for you out there, though."

"Maybe I'll get Mr. Hardcastle's number when we get the Caddy tomorrow." Cassie drifted in thought as she spoke. "*Reggie*."

Melinda smiled, a bit shocked. "The mechanic? Really? You would date him?"

"Why not? He is a good-looking man. There's no denying that. And he has his own business."

"Well, yes. But Cassie... he's a mechanic."

Cassie leaned in over the table. "And I'm in need of a good lube job, my dear."

Melinda let out a loud chirp of laughter. "Cassie! The things you say!"

"You should be used to all of them by now."

Melinda laughed into her coffee as she shook her head. "A mechanic? Really?"

AFTER Cliff had been sufficiently lashed for spilling his seed (and likewise David for causing said spillage), Mr. Scott thought it his Christian duty to read Leviticus to them. In actuality, Mr. Scott's voice via an old tape recorder did the reading. Mr. Scott had made his very own recording of the Bible—tapes and tapes of it—with some of the money Nanna had donated to the cause, and he was hoping to sell them to a publisher. They were all boxed up and ready to go in his bedroom. He was certain that his voice, no matter how antiquated the technology, would prove to be just the thing to de-gay the world. He would be heralded as a hero. He was obsessed with the notion.

The fact that Mr. Scott was unable to hear or accept, however, was that his voice was simply too weak a thing to make any sort of real impact, and his performance of the material was spotty. Every third word was hardly audible due in part to his lack of skill and in part to the poor quality of the tape and recording apparatus. The old man hadn't even a schoolboy's recording prowess. What Cliff and David heard over the Vagina Videologues was a muffled attempt at religious zeal.

In the morning, after a full night of Mr. Scott's blurry Bible-thumping, Sister Michelle came down to give the boys their daily portions of bread and water. This had been Newt's job, but when he could no longer be located, the job went straight to her. On a tray, she carried a large white plastic pitcher of water, a loaf of white bread, and a single glass. After going first to David, she set the tray down and took the gag out of his mouth.

"Thank you," he said calmly. "You look lovely this morning, Sister."

She said nothing. Her eyes showed no emotion at all. Neither compassion nor contempt. Maybe boredom. Maybe extreme boredom.

"Could we get some air fresheners down here?" David asked. "There is some strange rankness. Do you smell that? It's getting stronger. Cleanliness is next to godliness, or so they say."

She gave him a bit of the bread and a drink from the glass. The water spilled down his chin. She didn't dry him off.

"Thank you," he said again. "You're so kind. So gentle. Much more pleasant than the older pair. My mother always said you get more bees with honey than with bitter old people."

She looked him in the eyes as he spoke. Was she listening or looking through him?

"I think you would be a much better religious leader than Mr. Scott or Sister Sally. You have much more of a presence. And yet they have you doing the menial stuff like feeding us and taking out our shit. What's that about?"

Mr. Scott's muffled rendition of Leviticus continued in the background.

Michelle gagged David again and moved across the basement to Cliff. She set down the tray and took the ball gag out of his mouth. Sister Sally had sent her down the evening before to clean Cliff's belly of the spilled seed.

"My fellow sinner is correct," Cliff said between mouthfuls. "You are so much more of a presence than the old guy. So much more convincing. Your silence speaks volumes. I might even turn straight for you."

Blank stare.

"Mr. Scott is a grand talker, you see, and excuse me for saying this—because I know he is your friend and all—but he doesn't really have a lot to say, does he? He wastes words, don't you think?"

Michelle put the ball gag back into Cliff's mouth, then collected everything back onto the tray and walked to the stairs. She turned around once to look at them with a sort of grimace. Not a smile or a grin. A grimace. Both Cliff and David shivered. She left them to stare at one another, now slightly more frightened than they had been since arriving at their predicament.

VERA and Terrence sat with Becky in the hospital room. Terrence, wearing his Aquaman T-shirt, had wiggled his way onto the bed next to Becky. Vera, looking very Aurora Greenway, occupied a space at the foot of the bed, occasionally giving the patient's shins a supportive massage.

"Thank God your dad left to get something to eat," Terrence said. "I know I've hidden it well, but I have had just about all I can take of his reality show casting. He asked me earlier if I was on *Drag Race*! As if I would even need to compete."

"We've all seen you in drag," Vera said. "You ain't pretty enough for competition, baby."

Terrence gasped, more for show than from actual grievance. "It's a good thing we're in a hospital, bitch! Because one more comment like that and I'll—"

"M-hmmm." Vera caught him with her deadly condescension.

Becky was smiling. "Oh, I miss this! I want to be back home on Jasper Lane. I feel a bit like I'm in 'a very special episode.' You know. Those moments when sitcoms go all serious because of falling ratings

119

and they have a character come down with some bulimia or dyslexia. I hope I'm not an expendable character."

"Well, if you only have gas, you shouldn't even be in a hospital," Vera said.

"Yeah," Terrence agreed. "Fart it out like the rest of us. Just because you're pregnant don't make you special."

Vera shook her head. "Terrence! Be a lady, you vulgar little shit."

"Daddy doesn't want me to leave," Becky said. "I think he'd bar the door if I tried."

"You're a grown female woman!" Vera proclaimed. "If you want to leave, then leave. You can make your own damn decisions, can't you?"

"Yes. But one look into his eyes and.... He's so damn lonely and worried all the time since Mom died. I can't add any more to that."

"But, honey," Vera said, "he's got you in a cage, and you are letting him keep you there."

Becky shook her worry off. "New subject. Have you heard from Cassie or Melinda?"

"The Caddy quit on them in some little town with a hot mechanic." Vera brought forth her cell phone and showed a photo Cassie had taken of said mechanic on the sly. He was bent over the engine, and a thick vein snaked up his forearm as he was busy working on something. "They'll be back on the road to the camp tomorrow. There's been no word from Jason, though."

"And still no sign of David or Cliff?" Becky asked Terrence.

"No," Terrence replied. "Which is why Operation Rainbow Warrior goes into effect tonight. I'm going to go pay the Crazies a visit, and I'm going to get some answers if it kills them. I know they have something to do with this—them and their big obnoxious pink cross. I have all of Divine's films playing continuously at my house, and I am now one pumped-up and angry gay."

"Be careful, honey," said Vera. "You don't want to end up here in the hospital as well."

SuburbaNights: Vignettes from Jasper Lane

"I certainly don't!" he said, squirming. "That night last summer was quite enough."

"Wait! What happened last summer?" Becky squealed. "There is gossip from Jasper Lane I haven't heard yet? I demand to hear it!"

"Oh, honey!" Vera said. "Let me tell you all about it. I was there... for some of it, anyway. It was total debauchery. Total devastation and filth."

"Don't you dare!" Terrence protested dramatically.

"Our Terrence, our precious little fey one, got himself locked into a fucking machine and couldn't get himself out!"

"A what?" Becky asked.

"A *fucking* machine," Terrence said with a roll of his eyes. "Basically it's a dildo attached to a piston. You strap your legs in good and secure in whatever position you want to take it. There's a remote control that allows you to change the intensity of the fucking. I've heard it can be very hot. I just received it that day and was trying it out. But—"

"*His remote broke!*" Vera screamed. "I walked in on him—"

"You were spying on me! Cassie told you I had purchased it, and you were spying just so you would have a story to tell!"

"I was merely curious. A lady doesn't spy."

Becky was ready to explode with laughter. "What happened?"

"As I said," Vera continued, "I walked in, and there our poor Terrence was, on his living room floor, getting his ass hammered relentlessly by this *Terminator* fucking machine. I mean, he was literally being ridden around the room by this robot-with-a-dick."

Terrence sat beside Becky, lips pursed and arms folded.

"He was screaming, *'Vera! Help me! I'm being fucked to death!'* And Lord, I think he would have been if I hadn't been there!" Vera was now laughing and wiping away tears as she told the tale. "That thing was digging for gold. Well, it took some doing—picture me chasing him around the room in my best heels—but eventually I got it off him.

We came here immediately to see if any damage had been done to his pipes."

"And you laughed all the way here!" Terrence said.

"*I sure did!* I sure did!"

Both Becky and Vera were in hysterics. Terrence was, of course, put out. Just plain put out.

"It's not funny. I couldn't get fucked for three weeks after that! Three weeks! That was pure hell for me."

The commotion from all the laughter brought two nurses and Mr. Ridgeworth hurriedly into the room. Mr. Ridgeworth was not happy.

"You two, get out of here," Mr. Ridgeworth said. "Becks don't need all this chatter and roughhousing in her condition. Leave, both of you."

"But it wasn't me!" Terrence protested. "It was the mean black woman. Can't I stay?"

"I don't want to hear it, young man! *Out!*"

Mr. Ridgeworth grabbed Terrence by the arm and pushed him out the door. Vera followed, still laughing.

"You Hollywood types are all the same," Mr. Ridgeworth said. "Go find another reality show!"

"I'm not—" But the door was shut before Terrence could say anything more.

Of course, Becky would have said something to keep her friends near… if she had had the breath to speak.

THE trailer was a-rockin'.

Seth and Coby could not keep their hands off one another. Every free hour of the day they could manage it, they were grasping, poking, and sucking on each other until they were flushed pink and sweaty all over. Their relationship—whatever that was, though neither had named it—had at least evolved into something more interesting than a hookup after a workout. When Coby recommended they spend Seth's lunch hour in Coby's trailer, Seth was there with condom at the ready.

Coby lived in a boxy little camping trailer from the 1970s, all rust and silver. It was located in a trailer park on the very edge of the city, which, once Seth had driven there, only gave them around ten minutes to play around before Seth had to head back to work. But they made those ten minutes last. Even before Seth was completely inside the little trailer, Coby jumped him. Seth was bare-ass naked inside of ten seconds, and Coby was inside of Seth's bear ass five seconds after that. It was poetry how it worked so well. Seth's defeated He-Man cries were sheer music to Coby's play-villain ears. And while Seth had never been a bottom before, he was passionate about the position with Coby. Coby's dick was just the right length to unlock his tension.

In the end, after the sexual maelstrom, the tiny trailer was trashed. Anything that had been sitting upright was now broken and beyond repair. Even the trailer itself was lopsided from a busted axle due to the repetitive and severe hammering that had taken place inside. Everything not nailed down was now shifted to one side of the structure.

Seth grappled to quickly reclothe himself while keeping his balance in the tiny trailer. Coby sat naked on the broken tiled floor and watched his rugby star.

"I think I'm going to tell Rick I'm not in love with him anymore," Coby said, still in the after-thrall of lovemaking. He had grabbed a piece of fried chicken from the refrigerator and was hungrily stripping the meat from the bone.

Seth stopped dressing for a moment, his tie hanging loosely over his neck around the collar of his unbuttoned dress shirt. His dick hung out of his unzipped pants. He smiled like a jack-o'-lantern. "Why's that?"

Coby shrugged. "I think it's the truth. I'm over him."

Seth continued dressing. "Good."

"What about you? Are *you* over him?" He stopped chewing on the bone while he waited for an answer.

"I don't think I ever had it for him as bad as you did." He tucked his dick back in his pants and zipped.

"But you would still fuck him?"

Seth smirked. "Meh. I'm having fun with you."

Coby smiled and breathed deep. That was a good enough answer.

Seth, still not fully dressed, bent down and gave Coby a kiss. The trailer tilted a bit more. "I'll see you later tonight," he said. "I'll be back to help you fix this old heap you live in. Did you happen to notice that it's unbalanced?"

"Aren't we all?" Coby said.

Seth shrugged and then fumbled his way out the door.

"WE'LL be there in about an hour," James told Rick over the cell phone. James had been on the phone for twenty minutes in a hushed tone. It was the third time he had stated their ETA. "Yeah, baby. Of course I've missed you. I've missed you more than you know."

Had they been more alert, the wrestling team—every one of them drowsy in the back of the van—would have ragged James endlessly about his sentimental cell phone behavior. By now they had formed a nice bond with James, which meant teasing was allowed. Only good friends can point out your human inadequacies and still root for you at that very same moment.

The wrestling event had been filled with some pins and some wins, some hurt pride, some torn singlets, and one coming out. It had been a physical as well as an emotional roller coaster. The guys were plain exhausted and had been mostly quiet in the van all the way home. They listened to their iPods or simply dozed off as the evening sky fell and the number of passing car lights on the highway dwindled.

"Yeah, baby," James said, somewhat bashfully. "We can do that when I get home.... No.... Because I don't want to say that right now…. Because the coach is right here, baby…. Yes, I'd be embarrassed if he heard. That's our private sex language, baby…."

Coach Nipple flashed James a grin in the dark.

"See you soon. Love you." James turned off the cell phone and looked at the coach. "What?" he said. "Like you haven't had sexy phone talk."

"That was sexy?"

"All right. Flirty phone talk. But don't be fooled. Rick can be downright perverse sometimes. He looks innocent, but he can turn a phrase like it was a sex move."

"God bless the institution of marriage."

One of the wrestlers squirmed in his seat, trying to find a more comfortable sleeping position.

"Are you going to head that way with Melinda?" James asked.

"What way is that?"

"Marriage."

"Soonish? I'd say no. I'd be lying if I said I hadn't thought about popping the question, but I had to hold her hostage in that gas station just to get a date."

"What's the issue?"

"Honestly, I think she wishes I was… more."

"More?"

The dimming sky and passing headlights of other cars gave the moment a deeper poignancy. Suddenly the lack of any background music was blatantly apparent and they found themselves speaking in breaths.

"Like maybe she wishes I had invented the sport of wrestling instead of just being one of its coaches. She wants an honest-to-God prince. I think she's wondering if she can do better. She spent a lot of years with a lot of nothing. I can sort of understand her reluctance after being with Frank for so long. Sort of. But I think I'm worth it."

"I think the same about Rick sometimes."

"You wish he was more?" Malcolm passed James a surprised look.

"No. Just the opposite. I think he wishes *I* was more. I'm an army guy who inherited his uncle's estate. That's not too exciting."

"But you play rugby too. That's cool. That's a different angle."

James shrugged.

"Maybe we should tell *them* what we're thinking," the coach said.

"Maybe. I was just hoping I could get it all figured out so that Rick wouldn't have to do any of the work."

"Well," Malcolm said, "I can help you out a bit, I think. How would you like a permanent position with the team? The guys like you, and you seem to have a good time with them. It doesn't pay a whole lot, but as you said, you've got that inheritance to live off of. You ain't hurting."

"I would love it! It's something to do besides sitting around the house and looking up porn."

"Then you've got a job, fella. Congratulations."

The lazy sound of a single pair of clapping hands came from the dark at the back of the van.

"Congrats, Jimmy," one of the boys said—the one called Ted. "Now can you guys stop talking about your love lives? Some of us are trying to dream back here without thinking of your wrinkly old man balls slapping against somebody's ass."

"That just bought you fifty pushups when we get back home," the coach said.

"Fuck," came a mumble.

"Fifty more," said James.

The coach smiled and nodded to James. "We're going to make a great team."

"I'VE come to check on things, Mr. Scott."

Nanna Hench stood at the door, a cigarette in hand and the smoke curling from it in serpentine spirals. Mr. Scott was slack-jawed.

"Miss Hench," he sputtered, then gave a hard swallow. "Why, Miss Hench! We would have gladly told you over the phone how things were going. Yes, indeed. There was no need for you to come to see us. No need at all."

Nanna barged her way past him. Sally caught sight of the old woman, and they locked eyes momentarily. Sally, looking as if she had seen the true face of suburban evil, fled to the basement like a frightened chicken.

"I want to see with my own eyes what I'm funding here, Mr. Scott." Nanna motioned in the direction of the basement. "Is that where it's happening? Wherever that turnip of a woman scattered to? Is that where your aversion therapy program is located?"

"Y-yes, Miss Hench."

"Show me, then. And stop saying my name, silly man. Your voice annoys me."

Mr. Scott flinched as if he had been hit. "Excuse me, but I have been told I have a wonderful voice."

"You have been lied to. Now take me to the boys before my ciggy burns out. This is my last one, and I doubt I'll find any in this house, will I?"

Mr. Scott raced ahead of her and opened the basement door.

"You go down first," Nanna said. "I appreciate the chivalry, but I want something to catch my fall if my knees give out. You're not much, but at least you're something."

The steps creaked as they descended. A distinct odor made Nanna crinkle her nose as they approached the basement floor. The lights were on, showcasing everything. Nanna looked less than impressed. Much less.

Michelle and Sally stood in the center of the basement. Sally had a frightened yet prideful smile. Michelle expressed nothing.

The droning of Mr. Scott's voice reading Leviticus filled the room like a low rumble of nonthreatening thunder. Nanna walked forward, her face falling from one of utter disappointment to one of complete horror. There, directly across from each other, were two ratty mattresses, one holding David, the other holding Cliff—both naked, bound, and gagged. Nanna noticed their eyes go wide with recognition when they caught sight of her.

"Good Lord!" Nanna rasped. "Are you kidding me? Good Lord!"

Mr. Scott flinched again at her use of the Lord's name in vain… twice. Sally began to cower behind Michelle, inching backwards in small steps.

Nanna moved around to see what was being shown to David on the old television set. She went white when she saw the images of the naked women.

"What in all holy Hell is this?" she croaked, flinging her cigarette to the ground. She shook with fury.

"It's therapy," Mr. Scott said. "It's what you asked for. It's what they need. I told you my ways are controversial, but they *will* get results."

"It's perversion!" Nanna exclaimed. "You're just as bad as *they* are."

"Miss Hench!" He grabbed his lapels and stood straight. "I resent that implication."

"Resent all you want, you ignorant fool." She took the tape recorder and flung it across the room. It smashed against the wall. "And shut the hell up!"

Sally squealed.

"There's no need for such language, woman!" Mr. Scott proclaimed. "Or such violence. Now I'll have to get a new recorder."

Nanna approached him and he stiffened. "You listen to me, little man. This was not what I wanted. Kidnapping? With my money? Do you realize what these two boys could do to me if they get out and tell everyone where they've been? There are already posters around town with the big one's face on them."

"But they will be cured. When I'm through with them, they'll want to do nothing but thank you. Thank *us*! We'll be heroes to the cause."

She poked at his chest. "You find a way to get them out of this house. I don't care where. Just somewhere else. I'll figure out what to do with them after that. Clearly I've put my faith in the wrong man. Your therapy is a sham. I should have known better than to search on the Internet for help."

"It will work!"

She smacked him, and he fell to his knees. Sally screamed. Mr. Scott looked up at her with quivering lips.

"Get them out of here, Mr. Scott. I don't care how. Just get them out!"

Nanna turned around quickly. She gave Sally and Michelle a fleeting once-over. Then she looked at both Cliff and David. "Shit!" she spat out.

"Miss Hench!" Mr. Scott complained.

"The Lord would understand!" Nanna replied as she climbed the stairs.

MELINDA had chipped a nail. Not just chipped it, but nearly snapped the whole thing off as she was getting dressed for bed. It had caught on her satin nightgown—the one that made her feel more princess-like than any of her others—and *snap!* This was quite irritating for her for two reasons. Firstly, she loved that nightgown, and now there was an ugly snag in the pretty satin. And secondly, her nails grew at the speed of a lazy turtle on sleeping pills. Now that one of them was damaged, the rest of them would need to be cut back to match. (Melinda hated the tacky reputation of acrylic nails, so using them to balance things out never crossed her mind.) It would take another few months before her nails were grown out again.

When she searched through her purse, she couldn't find her pretty pair of clippers. She hardly ever had chance to use them anyway, so she wondered why she carried them at all. She remembered buying them years before when she had gotten a manicure. There was a lovely little painting on one side of the clippers, that of a little girl playing with a dog. Or was it a cat? Melinda wasn't sure. Honestly, she couldn't even remember using the clippers. Not once. Surely, at some point, she must have. But if she had, they weren't in her purse now.

Cassie never carried a purse. To see Cassie with a purse would be like seeing Terrence with a woman. But, Melinda thought, Cassie *was* the type of traveler who might bring along little comforts and almost-necessities like fingernail clippers. Maybe, with any luck, she had a pair hidden somewhere in her bags.

Cassie was in the shower, but Melinda didn't think she would mind if she did a little light foraging through her things in search of nail clippers. Women go through their friends' purses all the time.

It was almost immediately that she found the DVD Patrick had sent to Cassie. It was lying below a couple of T-shirts and a very elegant bra. She pulled the DVD out not to look at it but to see if there were any nail clippers beneath it. Sometimes smaller things get loose and shift to the bottom of bags. Her eyes took a moment to adjust to the sight of Patrick's face cracking a mischievous grin on the front cover. When she was finally able to take the entire image in—her son, half-naked with a group of completely whorish young hooligans, all standing beneath the title *Bros Bare All* and then the subtitle "Hot Nude College Boys Do Filthy Things With Inanimate Objects"—she clutched at her chest as if she was having a heart attack.

"No, no, no, no," she repeated as she grabbed Cassie's laptop and inserted the disc. "No, no, no, Patrick!"

But yes, yes, yes. Patrick Gold was right there in front of her on the screen. He looked as natural as could be. Not a hint of shame or embarrassment as he shed his clothes. He was in a hotel room somewhere and looked tanned and refreshed. He looked good on film.

Melinda jumped ahead on the disc, hoping a bit of ass cheek was all Patrick was going to show. But then....

The things he did with that roll of cookie dough!

"No!" she squealed, shutting her eyes tight and clenching her fists in a sort of fit.

She jettisoned the DVD out of the laptop and stared at the case in her hands, not knowing what to think. She hadn't heard Cassie come out of the shower behind her.

"Melinda," Cassie said, her hair still dripping wet. She was wrapped in a towel, with a look of true concern on her face. "I've been trying to tell you. He sent it to me the other day—"

"How could you?" Melinda screamed. *"How could you?"*

She dropped the DVD case on the bed and raced from the room in her nightgown.

"Oh, dear," Cassie said once Melinda had gone. "I'm so glad we're not hysterical people."

Cassie quickly dressed and went searching for Melinda but was unable to find her. After an hour she gave up and returned to the room, thinking Melinda would have the good sense not to go running around a strange town in her nightgown. She waited up. In Melinda's haste, she hadn't taken her cell phone. Eventually sleep won out and Cassie dozed off.

TERRENCE hid behind the big pink cross in the Jones's front yard. Standing there, he noticed that it already needed retouching. Served him right, he thought, for buying their paint at Walmart. No matter. He would need to paint it time and again anyway. At least until the Crazies had been driven from the Jones's house.

He was dressed in slim-fitting evening wear that blended him into the night. Terrence hated having to blend in anywhere, but he had no choice on this occasion. His evening wear this night consisted of a long-sleeved dark J.Crew turtleneck and matching pants. He even got a nice little black woolen cap for his head like he had seen them do in the movies.

"Dayum!" he had said when he looked in the mirror before he left his house. "Bitch! You are stunning."

He was as stealthy as he could be, slinking through the street seductively to his own inner music score. In fact, he was a bit too showy with his stealth, but there were so many Halloween decorations to hide behind, he was not seen. He smiled in self-satisfaction when he finally reached the cross.

"Now, to get in," he whispered.

He raised his binoculars. He didn't really need binoculars, but he had brought a pair anyway to complete the ensemble. Nothing completes an ensemble like binoculars. The lights were on in the house, but nothing could be seen through the thick drapes and blankets that blocked the windows. He groaned in disgust at the Crazies' lack of any perceivable taste, wishing there was someone else with him so he could make a sarcastic quip.

"I need a closer look," he said.

But then, just as he readied to move to the porch, he was betrayed. A beetle, a rather large one, most likely of demonic origin, had perched itself on one of the arms of the cross and began chirping quite loudly in a shrill continuous ring. Terrence yelped at once.

"Hush!" Terrence said. "Shut up, you! Shoo!"

But the bug did not move. In fact, it seemed to get louder, rubbing its hind legs in a *tsk-tsk* manner that only irritated Terrence more.

"Be off with you, silly creature!"

Terrence swatted at the thing, and, perhaps angered, it jumped at him. He screamed and brushed frantically at his clothes as he danced about the yard on his tip-toes until he was certain it was off him.

The door to the house opened a bit and Mr. Scott stood in the doorframe. Sally stared out from behind him.

"Who's there?" the old man yelled. "Get off my land!"

Terrence, already quite in the open, jumped onto the sidewalk with his chest out and his hands on his hips like some Dapper Dan Peter Pan. "It is I!" he said vociferously. "Terrence!"

Mr. Scott looked over his shoulder and grinned at Sally. He let go of his tight grip on the door. "It's the fairy," he said with a scornful guffaw. "I'll manage quite easily against him, I should think."

At the word "fairy," however, Terrence's whole demeanor changed from one of proud superhero to one of enraged queen. Terrence's hands fell from his hips and formed fists at his sides.

Before Mr. Scott could even focus his old less-than-worried eyes on Terrence again, Sally screamed and pointed. Terrence ran full force at Mr. Scott and tackled him into the house.

"My hip!" the old man cried. "You'll break my hip, you damn queer!"

This name-calling did not help Mr. Scott's plight. The two rolled around the floor of the mostly still unfurnished room, Mr. Scott trying to get away and Terrence making sure that didn't happen. Mr. Scott's white suit was being torn to shreds.

"I'm gonna beat your ass, motherfucker!" Terrence yelled. "You've pissed off the wrong gal!"

Mr. Scott screamed.

"This is for every gay kid in the world who's ever been bullied! *Tallulah!*"

(Of course, Terrence had meant to say "Tawonda," in reference to one of his favorite films, *Fried Green Tomatoes*, but he was so lost in the moment that all he could think of was "Tallulah," as in actress Tallulah Bankhead. Close enough.)

"Sister Sally!" Mr. Scott hollered between warding off punches. "Help me, you stupid woman!"

But Sally was of no help. She had screamed and run down to the basement before Terrence and Mr. Scott had even hit the floor.

133

She hurried down the steps in absolute terror. "Sister Michelle!" she cried. "Sister Michelle! Get them out! Home invasion! Home invasion! Get those boys up and out of here!"

Michelle looked at Sally blankly as she stood over David with a knife. She had untied an arm in preparation to move him and Cliff elsewhere. She seemed unconcerned with whatever was happening upstairs.

Sally ran to the exterior basement door that had recently been sealed up by Michelle and Newt.

"Quick!" she said as she moved the sandbags that had been placed in front of the plywood covering the door. "We have to get them out this way. We can't go upstairs. Mr. Scott—that brave man—is dealing with the intruder. Help me, Sister Michelle!"

Michelle moved forward but did not come to Sally's aide. She walked slowly toward Sally, staring at the back of the older woman's neck.

Sally looked at her. "Help me, you *stupid* little simpleton! Do something right for once in your life!"

Sally then easily pulled the plywood down. The homemade cement had not done its job of adhering it to the wall. It was, after all, basically just mud and oatmeal. Sally was at once hit by a terrible funk. She gagged and then covered her nose and her mouth. A couple of the large bricks that had been placed within the stairwell fell out, almost smashing Sally's toes.

"What in the world?" Sally said.

And then she saw the smashed face of Newt, his bulging eyes staring up at her, as clueless in death as he had been in life. She could not scream before Michelle was on top of her, wrapping her hands around Sally's throat.

David, realizing what was happening and seeing a chance to escape, had started to unbind himself the moment Michelle had her back turned. He worked quickly and was over beside Cliff by the time Michelle was struggling with Sally.

134

David and Cliff looked at each other with affection. *No time to kiss.* In no time, they were up, ignoring the need to stretch. They raced naked for the stairs and were at the top before Sally slumped dead to the ground.

Terrence was still fighting in the front room with Mr. Scott. The old man had gotten a good hit in here and there, but Terrence was still in a rage due to Mr. Scott's continuous homophobic rambling. The stupid old man didn't know when to shut up. Terrence was a bit surprised when, upon hearing a commotion from the basement stairs, he looked and saw David and Cliff, both nude, running towards him.

"Come on!" David shouted.

Terrence gave the old man a final whack, then jumped up and followed his two naked friends out into the night on Jasper Lane.

"My God!" Terrence yelled. "That was exhilarating!" He paused, looking at the naked bums in front of him. "Why are you both naked?"

"We'll explain later," David said as they ran. "Just follow us home, hero."

The Chapter in Which Cassie & Melinda Have a Fight

CLIFF and David were cuddled up with one another in a soft wool blanket, finally back in the living room of their own home. The morning light helped ease the tension, helped bring them out of the darkness. It was a quiet homecoming, though not without company. Rick and Terrence sat with them. They had done so all night. They flipped through magazines and TV channels.

Terrence's attack on Mr. Scott had shaken half the neighborhood. The sight of two naked men—one of them the size of a Buick—running down the street jarred everyone even further. Once back at their home, Cliff and David, still shaking, cleaned up and showered together while Terrence fixed them some coffee and a much-needed meal.

After calling Rick, Terrence tried Asha, who had been awakened by all the commotion. He told her what had happened in his usual gossipy manner.

"Are you on it, girl?" he asked as the bacon sizzled in the pan. "Are you on this for us?"

"I'm all over it," Asha said. "You just hole up in the house while me and my old partner go check things out at the Jones's place. We'll look around real good. I can tell when someone is hiding something just by asking a few questions."

When Rick first arrived at the front door, Terrence grabbed a spatula, ready for another smackdown just in case it was Mr. Scott coming to seek revenge. When Terrence saw it was Rick, he pulled his friend inside.

"We got some crazy shit going down on this street!" Terrence said. "I don't think there has ever been anything as nunchuck crazy as what I'm about to tell you...."

Once the four of them were together in the living room and Cliff and David had filled themselves up with Terrence's very early morning breakfast, the story was told down to its dirtiest detail. How Cliff was kidnapped. The Vagina Videologues. Sally's ogling. Mr. Scott's ogling. David's failed rescue. Cliff's wiener being smacked. Nanna Hench. Terrence's bully beat-down. It all came out in rushed sentences, each of them—David, Cliff, and Terrence—adding to the other's telling, and each of them marveling at the ridiculousness of it all. Of course, Terrence marveled the most.

"I just don't know what I'd do without you, Davey," Terrence choked out, his dramatics kicking in, though not without true heart. "Terrence without David is like... Big Edie without Little Edie."

Rick looked puzzled. "Excuse me?"

"A film reference." David smiled.

"Well, we're safe now," said Cliff. "Thanks to you." He held up his coffee mug. "To Terrence," he toasted. "The fiercest of all queens since Divine."

The others followed in the toast.

"Oh, hush," Terrence said. "It's not like they were going to kill you. They just wanted you to watch a lot of vagina videos. Torture akin to my experience in my junior high school sex ed class."

"I don't know about that," said David. His face was shadowed with concern. "That younger woman, Michelle... she was pretty dangerous. The others Cliff and I could have dealt with easily enough if we hadn't been bound. But Michelle? No. There was something... I saw it in her eyes just before we escaped. When she was untying me and Terrence was upstairs giving Mr. Scott his due, I thought for certain I was about to be gutted by her. And from what you found out about her past, Rick...."

"Do you think she killed that other woman? Sally?" asked Rick.

David looked at Cliff. "I'm sure of it. Asha will find the bodies of Newt and Sally in the basement if she can get a warrant."

"Lord!" exclaimed Terrence. "It's a *Nightmare on Jasper Lane*. Can you imagine? There was a serial killer living amongst us. You think you know your neighbors and one of them turns out to be Jacklyn the Ripper."

"I'm just glad to breathe some fresh air again," Cliff said. "It was getting rank down there." He gave David a hug that would have put a bear unconscious. "And I have never appreciated you more." He kissed his hubby ferociously. There was also some play happening beneath the blanket, which caused David to laugh.

"Hey!" Terrence chided. "None of that unless you intend to share. To the victor go the spoils, remember?"

"I'm looking forward to working out again," Cliff said. "I feel like I've wasted away to nothing. Are my boobies drooping yet?"

"It hasn't even been a week," Rick said.

"I know. An eternity."

"I'll love you, drooping boobies and all," David reassured Cliff.

"Gross," Terrence muttered.

The doorbell chimed. Terrence rose to answer, as protective as a bitch with puppies. He once again carried the spatula with him. By the tone of his voice upon answering the door, however, it was a friendly call. He walked back into the room with Asha. She wore an FBI hat and not a trace of makeup. She had a natural beauty to her that would have made runway models cry with jealousy.

"What news, Asha?" Rick asked.

"The house is empty," she said. "The door was open, so we went inside. There are some furnishings, but everything else is cleared out. Even the cross that was in the yard has been pulled up, if hastily. I think, whoever they were, they left in a hurry. The station wagon left some marks on the drive."

"Wait," Cliff said. "They got away?"

"Looks like it. Sorry, guys. The basement is a mess, though. There's an old TV there, a smashed tape recorder, and a couple of dirty mattresses."

"Nothing else?" David squirmed. "No... *bodies*?"

"Bodies?" Asha looked surprised. "No. Should there be?"

They were silent.

"Maybe you two should go to the authorities and make a statement. They can catch these freaks if they get the scent early enough."

"We will," David said. "Just not now. We need to rest."

"It's good to see the two of you are safe," Asha said. "Let me know if I can be of any more help. And if you need anything at all, don't hesitate to call Keiko. She loves you two."

They thanked her and she left, Terrence walking her out as if he lived in David's house again.

"What the hell does all that mean?" Rick said. "Nobody alive *or* dead in the house?"

"It means," answered Cliff, "we're going to have to be looking over our shoulders. And not just me and David. They had it in for all of us."

"YOU'VE been awfully quiet this morning, Miss Gold," Cassie said. "Aren't you going to speak to me?"

The road signs kept track of the tension. Every minute stretched for miles. They had been on the road for close to an hour. Cassie had found Melinda in the hotel lobby, lying sacrificially like Ophelia on the lounge sofa. Melinda hadn't said a word. She didn't acknowledge Cassie's presence then or now. She hadn't even looked Cassie in the eyes when they went to get the Cadillac. Her mouth was shut tight and her eyebrows seemed frozen in mid-condescension. The look was reminiscent of the Melinda she used to be. The Melinda Cassie had no desire to get to know.

"Say something, for God's sake." Cassie stared straight ahead as she drove. "You know those feathers I said I had lost? Well, it seems I was wrong. They're not completely gone. I'm getting a little ruffled right now, and you're the one doing the ruffling. What the hell is wrong with you? You make me sit through that *awkward* breakfast this morning where you did nothing but sip on your coffee and stare out the window while I prattled embarrassingly on, and then, when we pick up the Caddy, you won't even remark on how inferior Reggie is to me. Not even when I asked him out right in front of you. I did that for your benefit, my dear."

They passed a sign for the Straight To The Heart Reparative Clinic and Bible Camp. Cassie gasped in a mixture of relief and horror. She turned onto the marked road. They drove a bit farther down a gravel path lined with trees to a large but nearly empty parking lot. Cassie parked and turned to face Melinda.

"I'm not going to feel bad about this, Melinda," she said. "Patrick sent that naked college boy DVD to me for use at one of my porn parties. There was no other reason for it. And—before you even think it—no. I would have never shown it there. I tried to tell you about the DVD a couple of times, but you kept cutting me off with some terribly mundane thing or other. That's a habit you have, if no one has yet told you."

Melinda shot her a look of such death that it caught Cassie off guard.

"So it's my fault?" Melinda said. "This is all my fault?"

"Well, thank God you can talk!" Cassie exclaimed. "No. That is not what I said. There is no fault to be had here."

"Isn't there?"

"No."

"*Isn't* there?"

"Repeating the question with emphasis and crazy demon eyes won't make me change my mind, my dear. No. There is no fault here. Just a misunderstanding."

Melinda was staring ice-cold daggers into Cassie.

Finally, Cassie had had enough. "I don't know what the hell is wrong with you, darling, but we're here and I'm going to find my son. Come if you want."

Cassie got out of the Caddy. Melinda, quite flummoxed, yelled after her.

"How dare you just walk away from me!" she screamed. She got out of the car as well, then slammed the door with appropriate verve.

"Hey!" she yelled, catching up to Cassie. They walked up a grassy incline to a large authoritative-looking structure crowned with a cross. "Hey!"

"What?" Cassie yelled back, spinning around to face Melinda. "Can't this fit wait until later?"

"He's *my* son! Do you hear me?" Melinda clutched her purse strap as if it were a railing keeping her stationary.

"My God, Melinda! We've been over this before, haven't we? I know he's your son. What's that got to do with anything? I'm not trying to take him away from you."

"Why didn't he send *me* the movie? Huh? Why is it always you?"

"Well, I'm a bit shocked here. Would you want him to send you amateur pornography?"

"Of course not!" She shook her head in a fury, hair a-flying. "I just want the kind of relationship with him where he feels free to send me... those types of things if he wants to."

"Then do it! Who's stopping you from having that kind of relationship? Listen, my dear, I have enough issues with my own son. I certainly don't need to be juggling your fucked-up relationship with Patrick as well. If you want a stronger relationship with him, well, then, make one! Grow some balls."

Melinda's mouth dropped open. She reached out and gave Cassie's shoulder a light shove.

"Don't touch me, Melinda," Cassie warned politely yet sternly.

Melinda steeled her jaw and shoved Cassie again. "What are you going to do about it, Miss Bloom?"

Cassie showed her what she was going to do about it with a more violent shove that sent Melinda back a few steps.

"Calm yourself down, Miss Gold," Cassie warned.

Melinda threw her purse to the ground and prepared to begin the very first fight she had ever been in. She jumped on Cassie and went first for the hair, then tugged at the clothes, all the while making noises that were not very ladylike at all. Noises that came from her gut and sounded like a primitive beast.

"Really, Melinda," Cassie said. "Get ahold of yourself."

But Melinda grunted as she fell atop Cassie and they rolled down the hill, battling as best they could. Before long, however, Cassie's laughter was apparent.

"Stop laughing!" Melinda squealed. "Stop laughing, dammit. I'm kicking your privileged ass!"

This only incurred more laughter from Cassie until soon Melinda's fury had subsided and she too was laughing as she straddled Cassie's hips. She gave Cassie one more playful swat to the head.

"You win!" Cassie said, holding up her hands in surrender. "I give up. You are a better mother than me."

"No." Melinda tried to pick leaves out of her hair. "That's okay. I think we can safely share the title of Best Mother on Jasper Lane now that Sandy has moved away. She was our only real competition."

"For the time being, anyway. We just need to make certain Becky doesn't do a great job at it and we can keep that title."

They laughed, breathless and defeated.

"*Ladies!*"

A sharp voice invaded the merriment. A thin whistle of a woman—young with an old disapproving scowl—stood a few feet away with folded arms.

"Please!" the woman said. "We've had enough of *this* type of foolishness. Kindly get up and leave the premises."

Above her, on the hill, stood a motley crew of tired-looking people dressed in a similar fashion as she, all with yellow T-shirts that read the camp's name. A big shining halo hovered over the word "Straight."

Melinda got off Cassie, and they both rose to their feet.

"I'm so sorry," Melinda said, pulling a big dead leaf from Cassie's hair.

"Do you work here?" Cassie asked the indignant woman.

The woman gestured to her T-shirt, pointing out the obvious.

"I'm looking for my son, Jason Bloom. I heard he took a job at this ridiculous place. Have you seen him? Is he here?"

The woman's mouth quivered as if she would burst into tears. "He *was* here!" she yelled. "He's the cause of all of this."

"All of what?" Melinda asked.

"All of *this*. The camp! It's been totally destroyed. He and those little fruits who were sent here to be fixed went crazy. He was posing as normal this whole time. We trusted him. And then… *this!*"

Cassie couldn't hide her smile. Neither could Melinda. They didn't try.

"While I'd love to take a tour of the detriment caused by my son's awful behavior—"

"Just dreadful," Melinda chimed in with a wink at Cassie.

"—I really must find him. Have you any idea where he went?"

"How should I know?" the woman hissed. "He destroyed the place and left. They were like pillaging barbarians."

"Like Philistines?" Melinda offered.

"Yes! Exactly. Philistines! Don't think there won't be any charges! We'll get that lying sicko."

"Bring it on, girlie," Cassie said. "Oh. And one more thing."

"What?" sneered the woman.

Cassie reared back and hammered the girl's face, sending her to the ground with a cry.

"Don't ever offend a sicko's sicko mother."

"Whoops. Come on, Cassie," Melinda said, grabbing her friend's hand. "Let's go home."

As the other counselors ran frantically down the hill to see to the woman, Cassie and Melinda got into the Cadillac. Cassie, still shaking in rage, turned the ignition, but the car wouldn't start. She tried again, but nothing. She looked at Melinda and shrugged.

"My feathers have been ruffled," she said.

"We could call your new mechanic boyfriend to come fix it again?" Melinda said.

"No. We'll leave it here. I can get it later. I'll probably sell it anyway. I want to go home."

She paused to think, watching the panicked camp counselors run up the hill with their injured cohort, praying to Jesus as they went.

"We passed a small airfield a few miles back," Cassie remembered. "How are you with flying, my dear?"

WHEN Rick arrived home, he at first thought the house had been burglarized. The den had been cleared out, and the furniture was missing. But then, upon further inspection, he saw that things had just been moved to the edges of the room and a rubber mat had been positioned in the center. Leaning against the mantle in a blue wrestling singlet and white shoes, and proudly sporting a raging hard-on, was James.

144

"Wanna rassle?" James asked with a look that clearly implied no choice in the matter.

It was a stupid question anyway. Rick stripped down to his blue boxers. His hard-on was less successfully contained. Both he and James wore broad grins.

"You are going down, bitch," James said as they circled each other on the wrestling mat. "Down on *me*, that is."

"Yeah. I understood what you meant. No need to clarify. But you would be wrong."

"Rassle-mania!" James shouted wildly as he jumped on Rick.

Rick broke into laughter as they fell to the mat together.

"Winner takes all," James proclaimed.

"Up the butt," Rick corrected. "So I may just let you win."

James put Rick in a headlock, from which Rick quickly tapped out due to his inability to take the moment too seriously. Soon, however, Rick had the upper hand as he pinned James's arm behind his back. He lay on top of James and bumped his stiff erection into James's singlet-protected bunghole.

"Thwarted!" Rick said.

"And that's not the only fancy trick I've got up my sleeve," said James as he wriggled free of Rick's trap and flipped him back onto the mat.

James got Rick in another lock, only this time Rick's head was between James's thighs. Rick took the opportunity to have a snack, just a nibble on James's dick. He hadn't eaten all day, after all. While Rick sucked the meat through the singlet, James let himself relax. *The fool!* Rick used that moment while James was yet unaware to mount his counterattack, and began tickling James until he was free of the penis thigh trap.

"You cheat!" James howled as he rolled around on the mat.

Remembering the wrestling moves he had seen as a kid on the Friday-night TV programs, Rick intended to grab James by the seat and flip him. Instead, he hooked his thumb into James's bunghole.

"Forced entry!" James cried, his voice hoarse from laughing. "Foul!"

He turned the game about and meant to flip Rick in the same way. Rick's shorts tore off midlift. The now naked and flushed would-be victor fell to the mat, his dick more needy than ever. Rick reached around and grabbed a handful of singlet on each of James's obliques and pulled up as hard and as far as he could.

"Wedgie!" James screamed. "You win! I give! You win!"

James rolled away, his laughter slightly more damaged than Rick's. After a moment where they gathered themselves and summoned normal breaths, James rolled back to Rick and rested his head on Rick's shoulder as they lay on the mat. James reached down and took a firm grasp of Rick's dick.

"What are you doing?" Rick asked

"Winner takes it all up the butt, remember? Your rules. I want your butt."

"I don't remember saying that. What a ridiculous lie."

"Well, either way, your dick looks like a puppy begging for some love. Look at how it's staring at me." He changed his voice so that it was shrill and smallish. *"Please, James. Please suck me! I'm so very lonely down here."*

"I'm sorry it's so damn whiny. Jeez! What a voice."

"That's okay. I'll shut it up."

James crawled to Rick's waist and began playing with the thing, licking the slit and then circling his tongue around the glans.

"Make it cry, baby," Rick said. "Make it cry."

And James devoured it.

MR. RIDGEWORTH stood at the foot of Becky's hospital bed with a tiny Asian woman in pink scrubs. The woman's round face was cupped by a short severe hairstyle that was cut so perfectly it resembled a wig. She looked at Becky with an air of authority, as if she were looking over a wall and down at someone on the other side.

"Becks," Mr. Ridgeworth said, "this is Miss Lo. She will be looking out for you, honey. I need to get back home. Who knows what your brothers have gotten up to on the farm. I hate leaving them in charge of anything. I wanted to find someone who I thought would do a bang-up job at taking care of you while I wasn't here. I looked all over town, and Miss Lo is the ticket."

"Daddy," Becky replied, giving her eyes a rest from the gossip magazine in her lap, "I'm not going to be in the hospital forever."

"I know that, baby girl. That's why she'll be heading home with you when you leave here."

"No. Daddy, that is out of the question! I have so far given into all of your requests, but not this. Absolutely not." She looked at the woman. "Miss Lo, I'm sure you are a wonderful nurse, but… just, no. I can take care of myself perfectly well."

Becky resumed her reading.

Miss Lo looked at Mr. Ridgeworth with a questioning expression. She had yet to say a word. Mr. Ridgeworth neared his daughter and sat down on the bed beside her. He brushed a strand of hair out of her face.

"Now, Becks," he said, the gentle old dog showing his sad eyes, "it would make me feel a whole lot better knowing that there was someone with you in that big old house while you are in this condition. And there is plenty of room for her. I know you think you've got everything under control, but you're going to have a baby now. Things are gonna be different. Especially once it's born. You'll at least need a nanny. You don't plan on quitting your job, do you?"

"Of course not. I can't afford to quit."

"And who is going to take care of the child when you're at work? That television star? I don't think so. You'll need a proper nanny then, just like you need a proper nurse now."

"Daddy, I don't need someone looking after me all the time, watching my every move. Besides, my friends are right next door. And despite what you think of Terrence, he's been a good father to Christian."

"Sure. It's easy after the kids are grown. Terrence didn't actually raise his son, did he? Becks, this is going to be a full-time gig on top of your full-time gig."

Becky felt her resistance crumbling.

"She won't be hovering around all the time," Mr. Ridgeworth said. "Only when you need her. The woman is tiny anyway. How much space do you think she's going to take up?"

Becky sighed. "You know I'm going to give in, don't you?"

"That's because you're a smart gal." He kissed her forehead. "I raised you with a good head on your pudgy little shoulders. Now, I gotta get back home, baby girl. There are some things that need tending to, and your brothers are more trouble than blessings lately. Promise me you'll stay in the hospital for a couple more days. I don't think they'll force you to leave if I keep stuffing them with money. There's no plague."

Becky made no such promise, but she smiled to make it seem she had.

Mr. Ridgeworth and Miss Lo stepped out into the hospital corridor to discuss matters more thoroughly. Miss Lo's voice was an accented mumble. Becky reached for the phone beside her bed.

"I will *not* miss tomorrow night's Halloween party," she said under her breath as she dialed a number. She waited for the pickup on the other end.

"Hi, Vera," she said. "I am in desperate need of your help. What are you doing before the party tomorrow?"

TERRENCE proudly led the Mean Girls in an impromptu performance in the front yard of his house. This was in gaudy celebration of finding David and Cliff. Terrence had made all the Girls jealous by explaining to them just how exactly his handsome friends had been found, as in naked and running. (Much lip-licking and near wrist-spraining occurred in the privacy of their own homes as a result of this information.) When Terrence heard from Rick that James had been offered a new job with Coach Nipple, he added that to the list of things to celebrate as well. Thus, the alcohol was doubled. Of course, it would have been anyway.

The queens were a mess before they even began. They seemed too disjointed to do anything cohesive. One of them—Liza—had a smear of lipstick across her face, and she hadn't even had a drink yet. When Terrence pointed this out, Liza responded that she was going for a more daring new look.

Terrence yelled like a stage mother. "I'll give you a daring look if you don't clean that mess up, Courtney Love!"

The queen rolled her shaded eyes. "Watch your relevance, bitch."

For an audience, there were James and Rick, Keiko and Asha, and David and Cliff. They sat in lawn chairs that had been scattered across the yard. Terrence had apparently been expecting a whole theater room of people to show for the performance. He got six and a dog.

Rick turned to David and Cliff before the catfight ended and the show could begin. They sat in the row behind him and James. "You two should be resting," Rick said. "We'll keep an eye out for any weirdness in the neighborhood."

"We can't sleep," David replied. He was leaning back, his legs wide apart and an arm draped over the back of Cliff's chair. "Besides, we didn't want to miss the show."

"What do you think of it so far?"

"They're working the skirts."

"True. There are some nice legs in the group."

The Mean Girls continued prepping, twirling and doing the splits as if these moves were even part of the routine.

"I don't know how I feel about the string thongs beneath the skirts, though," said Rick.

Terrence was still arguing with Liza/Courtney Love. His hands were on his hips and he was pecking like a hen. Eventually, after a few more screeches and insults, he got his way and the queen washed her face with water from Terrence's water bottle.

"I remember the first time he screamed at me like that," David said. "It was back in college. For his birthday I bought him a scale. He had been wanting one to keep himself on some silly all-liquid diet that caused him to urinate excessively."

"He was offended by that gift?" James asked, turning around to join in the conversation.

"No. He loved it when he first saw it. He gave me a big kiss on the cheek. But then he saw what I had done to it." David grinned. "I had one of my more craft-savvy friends take it apart and replace the scale numbers with the numbers one through six. Then I had him warp it so that the scale stuck on six. And above the numbers I had engraved the word *Kinsey*."

"Yes. Very funny!" Terrence broke in amidst the snickers. "You're so very clever, David. A Kinsey Six. Ha, ha. Now, can we get on with our show? Or are there other episodes from my past you would like to chat about?"

"Sorry, Terrence," David said. "You just make it so easy."

Terrence turned to the queens with a huff. "Ladies," he said, "let's begin!"

Everything went well… at first. They were in rhythm and in sync with the music—a dance piece that used tribal elements and curse words mixed with Dolly Parton songs—and they really seemed to enjoy themselves. They ground their hips and crotches and rubbed against each other quite zealously. Their human triangle was a thing of sheer beauty despite a slip of the finger that caused Terrence, who was at the pinnacle, to squeal. But just a little.

And then it all came crashing down. Gayhound, that exuberant and curious doggy, tried to climb the pyramid himself. Glitter hadn't hit the ground that hard and fast since Mariah Carey.

Rising from the heap of drag queens, Terrence was irate and blamed the whole thing on The Artist Formerly Known As Liza. Gayhound barked and wagged his tail furiously, seemingly thinking it was all a bunch of fun as Terrence and Liza screamed at each other over the music. The rest of the Mean Girls, however, were less bothered by the whole ordeal and seemed to be rather relieved it was all over. They got up, dusted themselves off, fixed their tits, and danced.

The audience laughed and clapped, shouting cheers of "Good show" and "Encore." All except Cliff, who sat completely oblivious to what had just occurred. Arms folded across his chest, he stared into space. He didn't even move when Gayhound ran to him and begged for some lovin'.

"Are you okay, baby?" David asked, having suddenly lost interest in the Mean Girls and their stage mother.

"Yeah," Cliff replied on waking. He didn't look at David. "I'm good. I think I'm just going to go work out. Okay?"

"Sure, baby. But…."

David watched, his face hung with concern, as Cliff rose and walked back to their house.

"Is everything okay?" asked Rick.

"No," answered David. "I don't think so."

CASSIE had booked Melinda and herself a flight back home in a small engine plane. It was midafternoon when they arrived at the tiny airport they had passed earlier. They followed the pilot, Joanna—a woman as cool and certain as could be imagined, and with a strut to impress the mob—across the tarmac. The sun was out. The breeze was easy. It was a good day to fly. Theirs was the only flight scheduled for that afternoon. Joanna said, in her cocky daredevil manner, that she was happy to have something to do, "else I'd be bored here until tomorrow. Don't have anything till then."

She looked at Melinda and winked.

Melinda was nearly in giggles as she and Cassie followed Joanna. "I can't believe what we're doing!" she said. "It's like I've got my own private plane. 'Where's your Cadillac, Melinda?' 'Oh, I just left it behind. I can always get another.' The ladies at the city council would be so jealous. Not that I care what any of them think. But, do you think we can get a photo?"

"I don't see why not," Cassie said.

A slight vibration in her hip pocket let Cassie know she had a cell phone call. She looked at the caller ID and came to an abrupt stop. "It's Jason!" she gasped. "Oh, my heart!"

She held up her hand to Joanna in gesture of "one moment" and took the call. Melinda and Joanna went on ahead and waited for her by the plane. Melinda molested the body of the small plane the moment she reached it. Joanna was more than happy to give her a tour of the exterior.

"Jason!" Cassie said. "It's about time I heard from you. Are you okay?"

Thank God there were no other flights to make it harder to hear. The phone reception was terrible as it was.

"Hi, Mother," Jason said, as calm as if he had just seen her an hour before. "I'm fine. A lot has happened."

"I've heard. Melinda and I have been looking for you. We just came from that horrid camp your father wanted to send you to. You've made a mess of things there, haven't you?"

"Are you angry, Mother?"

"Of course not, sweetie. I couldn't be more proud of you. But I am worried what you've gotten yourself into. There may be legal problems ahead."

"I expected that. I'm not worried. We've got enough info on that camp to bury them and maybe even get some prison time for the assholes who run it. The things they were doing there, Mother… it was torture."

She heard his voice crack, and it made her sick to think of him so upset. Sicker still to think about what he had seen of his father's plans for him.

"Jason, hurry home, will you? I want to see you as soon as possible."

"I'll be home soon… and with some friends, if that's okay."

"Friends?"

"Mother," he said, "do you think we could renovate the basement?"

"The basement? That wretched place? What do you mean? Renovate it into what?"

"Like a gay hostel or something? Maybe a halfway house for gay runaways?"

Cassie smiled. "I think that might be something we could look into, yes."

"Excellent." He sounded very relieved. "I have nine kids with me who are in desperate need of a place to stay—for a place to feel safe—just for a few nights."

"That sounds wonderful. Bring them by. They can stay for as long as they want."

"Good. We'll be there by tomorrow evening. Just in time for your Halloween bash, if I'm not mistaken. Sorry if we don't have the time to go costume shopping."

Cassie put her hand to her chest and breathed deep in relief.

"I gotta go," Jason said. "Love you, Mother. We'll see you tomorrow. Goodbye."

"Love you.…"

With tears, she turned and looked at Melinda and Joanna. Melinda waved her forward.

"Let's get that photograph taken," Melinda said. "I want to remember this day."

Cassie wiped her eyes and walked up beside Melinda. She put an arm around Melinda's shoulders while Joanna took the photograph.

"Me too," Cassie said.

LOOKING for an extreme hardcore workout, Cliff chose to tempt an aneurism by heading to Shred Headz Gym, where the other heavy-duty bodybuilders and power men lifted. On the sensory level, it was not the most appealing of places. This pit of testosterone smelled like a locker room, and the locker room smelled like rotten eggs. But for the encouragement of sheer animal rage, it was the place to be. It was legendary. Nothing was breakable at Shred Headz because everything had already been broken. Every dumbbell, every bench, every plate in the place had survived by being the strongest and most durable. It seemed every light in the gym, no matter how new, had achieved age just by being there and so gave an automatic dimness. The banging and cranking of the weights and equipment, combined with the yells and grunts of the terrifying men there, gave Shred Headz an angry industrial feel. Grit, rust, and lust. No music allowed.

Though Cliff was the only openly gay man working out at the moment—rumors abounded about all of them, of course—the place was so humid with perspiration it might as well have been a twenty-four-hour man orgy. The sweaty muscle worshippers were, quite literally, tasting each other for the whole of their workouts. A few of the guys, knowing what line of film Cliff had been involved in and considering him a friend, constantly asked him questions about the gay porn process. At first they were merely curious, but when they heard the amount of money that could be made by spreading their legs and getting laid, the interest in the matter soared. Three of the Headz men—every one of them straight, as far as could be ascertained—even made appearances in some films, getting blowjobs from qualified specialists in the field of fellatio. One of them—a 'roid rager nicknamed Thumper—went even further. Cliff, on set for moral support at the time of Thumper's debut, had gotten a chuckle out of seeing Thumper's expression when he was finally eyed down by some top's savage dong. There was a mixture of fear, confusion, and awe on the newbie's face: *Fuck it, suck it, or feed it a peanut?*

It wasn't long into his workout that Cliff was forced to tell the guys what he had been through—the kidnapping, at least. They had noticed his absence, and a few of them had seen the large pink posters with his Xeroxed photo on them. Cliff knew he would not get away from them, especially Thumper, without explaining a little.

"Want us to clobber 'em for you?" a big hairy brute named Jarod asked. This was usually Thumper's workout partner.

"We'll grind him up real good," Thumper said with nasty vehemence. It was baffling how this easily addled young man with arms like tree trunks and a temper like a speared bull ever became a university professor. But apparently, he was good at his job. His students sometimes dropped by the gym just to see him. "Nobody treats our friend like that. I'd like nothing better than to pulverize this preacher man. I bet I could do it with my pecs alone. Just put his head between my tits and *kaboom* goes his head. What do you think?"

"No thanks, guys," Cliff said as everyone in the gym stood around his bench in a mountain range of soaked and steaming muscle. "I'll take care of it. It's my pride I need to get back, anyway."

"Pound 'em good!" Thumper shouted. "That's what you should do."

"You're gonna have to tell this story a couple more times," Jarod said. "There's a few guys who ain't here who'll want to hear it."

"This is where my friend Terrence would come in handy," Cliff said. "He and his cheer squad could come up with a production number explaining the whole thing. Then I wouldn't need to say another word about it."

"Yeah, but"—Jarod shrugged—"who would watch it? We're, most of us, straight dudes. If it don't got tits, we don't watch it."

"Pound 'em!" Thumper shouted once more, still in an inner tirade. Cliff had always thought Thumper resembled a more attractive version of Howdy Doody. His ears protruded from his head, taking the menacing edge off his scowl and his herculean body.

Coby entered the gym as the guys continued to probe Cliff with questions. Cliff saw him head into the rank locker room. He was waiting on someone, no doubt. Any one of the guys at Shred Headz could be a client of Coby's. Most of them had probably purchased from him. No sooner had Cliff seen the trailer park drug dealer than Thumper excused himself from the group with uncharacteristic discretion and retreated to the locker room as well.

"Well, we'll let you get back to it," Jarod said.

"Huh?"

Cliff hadn't really been listening to what the guys around him were saying. All he could think of was Coby with the steroids in the locker room.

"Your workout," Jarod restated. "We'll let you get back to it."

"Oh. Yeah. Thanks, guys."

The group of large men disbanded, and Cliff picked up a dirty brown dumbbell he had been curling at the outset. He tried to concentrate on his repetitions. His mind, however, was on other matters, and he was unable to bring it back.

MR. SCOTT flinched with every word from Nanna Hench.

He sat nervously on a floral couch in her apartment. It was a place much nicer than any he had ever owned. After all, the house on Jasper Lane was a rental. Nanna Hench owned that, having bought it under another name. Mr. Scott had, until then, lived in dingy apartments and bad neighborhoods.

Mr. Scott's hair was now dyed a ridiculous shade of auburn, and his clothes were homely and undistinguished. He was tense in them, as if he didn't want his skin to touch this lesser fabric of clothing. This was strange being that the outfit he now wore had been purchased at the same store from which he had bought his prized white suit. The suit, he had been told by Nanna Hench, that he must never wear again. Not if he wanted to blend in to a crowd.

Nanna walked back and forth in front of him, railing into her cell phone at the unfortunate caller on the other end. More bad news. Mr. Scott—terrified and stuttering—had already told Nanna about the escape of the two deviants known as David and Cliff, about the gruesome deaths of both Sister Sally and Brother Newt, and about Sister Michelle's sudden disappearance after they had stuffed the bodies in the station wagon and were preparing to leave Jasper Lane in the dead of night. Everything was falling down around them. What more could go wrong?

Nanna flung her cell across the room and then lit a cigarette. "Well, this is just a wonderful little turn of events," she said. "That was the head counselor at Straight To The Heart. Apparently that little *shit* Jason Bloom has betrayed us. That Judas! He and those little gay hooligans ransacked the place and took off for God knows where."

Mr. Scott put his shaking hands over his bruised face. He would never get over the shame of being beaten by a gay man. "Why has God forsaken us?"

"Because we're fools!" Nanna said. "We trust too easily. We wear our hearts on our sleeves for anyone to take advantage of. This world isn't meant for the likes of us, after all." She took a long contemplative drag on the cigarette.

Mr. Scott looked ready for a breakdown. "We just want to do right by the Lord, yes we do. That's all. Yes, it is."

Nanna looked him up and down. "Indeed," she said. "Tell me. Why do you talk like that?"

"Like what, may I inquire?"

"Like *that*, with all those unnecessary words hanging in strange places. Nobody strings together sentences like that. It's like they've been all messed up. Jumbled. Like the wrong end is up."

"I am certain I do not know what you are speaking of."

She gave a wave of the hand, letting him know she wasn't truly interested, only annoyed. "Anyway," she said, "we're going to need to rectify matters."

"But how? We are alone."

"Tomorrow night," Nanna said as she began pacing again with her cigarette, "Cassie Bloom has her annual Halloween bash. It's a sight to see. Everyone will be in costumes. It's a disgusting display. Demonic."

"The Devil's night!"

"We're going to organize a march on Jasper Lane. I'll get those people I know most trustworthy and closest to the cause to come along. You get the ones you know, if you know any. We'll even get those slackers from the camp to come as well. That's a good twenty people. More than enough to cause a stink. Me and you will meet somewhere tomorrow to get all the details hammered out." Nanna smiled between coughs. "They'll all be sorry they ever messed with Nanna Hench."

"Should we hand out Bibles?"

"What?"

Mr. Scott seemed once again excited. "At the march. Should we hand out Bibles?"

Nanna gave him a look of extreme annoyance that made her resemble a more ancient Yoda. "Good God! You're a moron!"

AT THAT very moment, a taxi pulled onto Jasper Lane. Out of the backseat emerged Cassie Bloom and Melinda Gold. They retrieved their luggage and stood for a moment, looking at the cul-de-sac, as the taxi drove away. Everything was quiet.

"I have a feeling we've missed quite a bit while we were gone," Cassie said. "Vera was telling me there's been some excitement."

"I'm sure we'll be filled in soon enough."

"Do you want Patrick's DVD?" Cassie held the case out to Melinda.

"No. Thank you, but it was his gift to you. I do plan on calling him tonight, though. I think we need to discuss some things, he and I."

"I won't watch it. I promise. I have no desire to see innocent Patrick baring all."

Gayhound rushed to them, barking happily and wagging his little gay tail. He jumped up for Melinda to pet him.

"Are you ready for the party tomorrow night?" Melinda asked Cassie as she rubbed Gayhound behind his ears.

"I will be." Cassie turned and smiled at Melinda. "Thank you for coming along. It meant a lot."

Melinda gave her a hug. "I'll see you tomorrow," she said. "Thanks for the plane ride."

They parted, Melinda with Gayhound in tow to her lovely home and Cassie to hers.

Eric Arvin

The Chapter With the Halloween Party

HALLOWEEN on Jasper Lane and, as usual, the neighborhood had gone all out. Ghosts hung from trees, jack-o'-lanterns the size of small cars smiled at passers-by, scarecrows lounged on bales of hay in front yards, and zombie attacks—because one can't step out their door without seeing a zombie these days—were depicted with some skill in various stages of mastication. Cassie Bloom's house, high at the end of the Lane, looked every bit the ghostly mansion, draped just that morning in an all-encompassing eerie "creepy old house" fabric. The manse was now masked.

The walkway up to the deck was now adorned on either side with sickly twisted trees that seemed intent on reaching out and snaring the party guests-to-be. There were also dancing skeletons, swinging bats, and cackling witches, all accompanied by the low background moaning of spirits and demons. It was as excessive as the holiday itself. For the night, Cassie had even employed several of Vera's boys from the club to walk around as beautiful half-dead, half-naked servers. No one was to be denied their meat on a stick.

It was noon, and, having worked most of the morning setting things up, Cassie relaxed with Vera and Melinda on the deck—now a funeral parlor and wake complete with a coffin that would soon be filled with ice and an assortment of alcohol.

"I heard, Miss Melinda," Vera said, playing with her gold bracelet nonchalantly, "that Nanna Hench is going to be on the march tonight."

"Here?" Melinda nearly dropped her coffee. "What?"

"That's what I heard. While at the Little Gay Book Nook, one of my boys was accosted by some religious deviant and handed a Xeroxed flyer."

Vera pulled a small pamphlet from her large purse and handed it to Melinda.

Melinda put a hand to her forehead and rubbed. "Oh, that woman. I'm so embarrassed! She's going to picket the Halloween bash? I'm so sorry, Cassie."

Cassie chewed on a bat-shaped wafer. "Why? She's not your mother. I'm the one who should be embarrassed by all of this. In fact, I think I will be. Yes. I've decided this very moment. I am in fact very embarrassed right now."

"Why is that, dear?" asked Vera. She tipped back a martini.

"Well, it's a matter of show, isn't it? You know the crowds Nanna draws. Or the lack of them, I should say. I'll be utterly humiliated if there aren't more than two hundred people protesting down there. Just flat-out humiliated! There is no way Nanna Hench will draw a crowd like that. For the things I do, I deserve to start a riot every day."

Melinda smiled. "Really, Cassie. You're too much sometimes."

"No. I'm serious. This party is going to be massive. Absolutely, revoltingly huge. The cops will be called at least twice. Everyone will be here. *Everyone*. From all around the city. And, let us not forget, my Jason is coming home."

Vera gave a brisk applause.

Cassie continued. "Yes. This will be a grand affair. We shall disturb the peace and then laugh when they chide us for it! Nanna Hench better bring her Rogaine."

Melinda, puzzled: "You mean her 'A' game?"

"That's what I said. 'A' game."

"You know, my dear," Vera said, placing her hand on Melinda's, "David tells me that Nanna had something to do with his and Cliff's captivity. You should hear what went on down in that basement. Twisted stuff."

161

"It seems Nanna is not the woman we all thought her to be," Cassie said.

"I can't act surprised," said Melinda. "It makes sense somehow that she would be behind all of this. I wish David and Cliff would press charges. Maybe we as a street should do it, just to keep her away. If she doesn't own property, she has no right to be here."

"She *has* caused enough trouble. That's for damn certain." Cassie stuck another wafer in her mouth. "And then there's the possibility of the murders in the basement. There will be some ghost stories popping up from those rumors. By next Halloween I imagine the house will be on one of those haunting tours."

"Our very own ghost story… if it's true." Melinda shifted in her seat. Her eyes grew big as she thought on the matter. "I mean, can you imagine? Someone dead and buried right under our noses."

"Imagine that," Cassie said. She gave Vera a quick wink.

"If there was a murder in plural form," Vera said, "I just hope they don't try to haunt any of you who live here. Or me, for that matter, when I'm too sauced to go back home. There's nothing worse than a self-righteous spirit."

The street below bustled with people admiring decorations. There were even a few children from other streets. Jasper Lane was always a big draw on Halloween.

"When is Becky coming home from the hospital?" Melinda asked. "I need to go visit her. She's not going to miss the party, is she?"

"Oh, no. She'll be here," Vera said. "There's no need to make a trip to the hospital to see her. I'm going to go… pick her up shortly."

"That's a very devious grin you have there, Vera," said Melinda.

"These be devious times, my dear."

COBY'S trailer was once again a lopsided tin can of lust. The differentiation in angular direction was an impediment to Seth as he tried to squeeze into the Halloween costume Cody had bought for him to wear that night. When his balance was in question, he could not dress as rapidly as he got undressed.

"I don't know about this," Seth said. He stood in front of Cody's tiny bed, a large hairy rugby player in a constricting maid's costume. "I've never done drag. I'm an ugly woman. And this is so damn tight."

Coby's expression was not encouraging. He itched at his head. "Yeah. It doesn't fit you very well at all, huh? Not even in that sexy goofball way."

Seth's arms jutted slightly out from his sides. "I can't even relax. If I do, I'll tear the zipper in the back and the whole thing will fall off. I think this is a woman's outfit, dude. Not a drag queen's."

He lost his balance and fell to the bed.

"It's all I could afford, baby," Coby said. "Sorry."

It felt strange to be calling someone "baby" again.

"I told you I would pay if you really wanted to get dressed up," Seth said. "I've got the money."

"No." Coby was adamant. "I am taking responsibility. From here on out I want to do things right. That means buying my own way through life, even if that makes me stinking poorer than I am."

Seth leaned in and gave Coby a kiss on the tip of the nose.

"Why do we even need costumes?" Seth asked. "We're not going to be spending a whole lot of time out tonight, are we?"

"I don't know. I just figured everyone else will be in costume so we should be too." He looked at the hot dog costume he had bought for himself, which was hanging on the bathroom door. In truth, he had never been a costume guy. Not every gay man likes dress-up. "But I don't really want to wear that. And you look ridiculous in what you've got on. Maybe we could just head to Cassie Bloom's party, do what we're going there to do, and then come on back here."

"I think that sounds like a much better plan. We'll have a night full of euphemisms."

163

Coby reached under Seth's skirt. "Well, I can think of a whole lot of euphemisms, so we should get started right away."

As they kissed, they were interrupted by a pounding on the door of the trailer, causing it to shake. A heavy voice hollered out "Coby! I'm here to collect what you owe me. I know you're in there."

Coby's skinny face went skeleton white. "Shit!" he said. "He's going to kill me!"

"Who the hell is that?" asked Seth.

"Just a big bruiser. I owe him. I owe him big. His temper is the reason Rick lost an eye way back when. What the hell should I do, Seth?" He clutched the blanket on the bed as if it might offer some defense. "There's nowhere to hide. Nowhere to run."

Seth rose. "I'll take care of this," he said. He brushed the wrinkles from his ill-fitting skirt and walked to the door.

"Seth, no!" Coby said. He hid beneath the blanket when Seth opened the door.

The angry man knocking—short and round, resembling a bleach-dyed bullfrog—took a step back when he saw Seth.

"What the—? Who are you?" he asked, giving Seth a judgmental once-over.

Seth took on his most intimidating rugby stare and tensed his body as if ready to go get that ball. He knew that it didn't matter what clothes one wore. Intimidation was the key.

"I'm the help," he said.

The collector swallowed. "Listen. I don't want no trouble. Just tell Coby to get on out here so we can talk."

"What you wanna talk to him for?"

"That's between me and him."

"Wrong. What you wanna talk to him for?"

Seth knew how to look as big as a house. A small trailer was kid's play.

"He owes me money, see? We had a deal. I'm just here to collect on that deal."

"You'll get your money when I get mine. Now git."

"Hey now," the collector said, daring to step closer. "I came here for my money, and I intend to leave with it."

Seth let out a low growl, and the collector backed off a bit. "No, sir," Seth said as he descended from the trailer like a god of war from the sky. "You'll leave now or else I'll be crushing your big thick skull."

"Now, listen you—" The collector was retreating before he realized it.

"Git!" Seth bellowed.

An angry hairy man with legs the size of tree trunks, a snarl like a wolf, many missing teeth, and the stare of a possessed pit bull would have been scary enough. But one also wearing a tiny maid's uniform was just insane. The collector scampered for his El Camino and quickly sped away. Seth knew he would be back, but there was no use worrying about that now.

Neighbors came from their trailers to see what all the hubbub was about.

Coby came out of his tin can with the blanket tied around his waist.

"That was amazing," he said. "Nobody's ever done anything like that for me before."

He slid a folded bill into the top of Seth's maid uniform.

"What's this?" Seth said, reaching in and pulling the bill out.

"For your troubles," Coby said with a grin.

Seth laughed. "It's not even real!" He unfolded the Monopoly money.

Coby shrugged. They kissed.

Before heading back inside the trailer, Seth turned to the neighbors who were still gawking. "What?" he yelled.

They fled back into their homes.

AS DAVID took his first afternoon jog since his escape from religious oppression, it was not the imaginative and gory decorations of suburban America that nearly made him trip and fall. Nor was it that vicious root on Parry Drive. No. In fact, it was a shockingly horrid auburn dye job that caught David's eye just two streets away from Jasper Lane. The hair may have been dyed, the white whiskers may have been shaved, and the old Colonel Sanders suit may have been traded in for ill-fitting work clothes, but it was most definitely Mr. Scott whom David saw as he jogged near Peter Park. What was more, Mr. Scott was sitting, albeit uncomfortably, with the unmistakable form of Nanna Hench. She too had tried to dress so as not to attract attention. She might have pulled it off if it weren't for the Halloween wig she was wearing. It resembled her own head of hair too much.

Nearby, David found a big white van with tinted windows and hid behind it. He watched as Nanna seemed to get very agitated, puffing on a cigarette as smoke rose from every orifice in her face. Mr. Scott looked like a frightened (and frightening) clown. Literally. That hair! It made him look like an ogre to Nanna's dragon. David watched the pair closely, feeling the anger spike in him, until the two conspirators rose, looked around, and then departed from the park in opposite directions.

Denying himself vengeance for the moment, David hurried back to Jasper Lane. He decided it would be best for his and Cliff's relationship—and sanity—if charges were leveled against Nanna and Mr. Scott. Somebody had to pay for what he and Cliff had been through. He was going to get dressed, shower, and go downtown to file.

When he arrived home, he saw Cliff sitting stoically on the front porch swing. He had been stoic a lot since the escape. Even their sex hadn't had the usual flair. The big man didn't seem to register David's arrival, so lost in thought was he. There was a time when Cliff had beamed at the first sight of David. Cliff wore a V-neck T-shirt and comfortable blue sweatpants. David took the seat next to him on the swing.

"It's a little chilly," David said. "You should get a sweater."

Cliff only nodded as if he'd consider the idea, but it seemed an automatic response. The swing creaked and whined.

"This is a stupid question," David continued, "but are you okay?"

Cliff broke his vacant stare and looked at David. "It's not a stupid question. There's just not a simple answer to it."

"We'll get them, baby. I just saw Mr. Scott with Nanna at Peter Park. They were talking very suspiciously, probably planning something ridiculous and sure to fail. I'm going to go file a report on the incident. The moment they set foot on Jasper Lane, we've got them. Maybe we'll even get to land a few punches before they get carted off."

"That would be fun. But that's not what's on my mind."

David began massaging Cliff's leg. "Then what is it?"

"Being there in the basement, unable to do anything… it made it even more real to me how lost I am."

"Lost?"

"I'm not my best." His voice was cracking. "Not for you *or* me. All my life I've glided on my looks and my… talent. But I want to be the best Cliff I can be, and it suddenly occurs to me that I have never been the best Cliff. I've never even tried. How do I do that? How do I become better? Did you know I never graduated from college? I went one term and then dropped it because of the crazy money I was making being fucked. But now that that's over, I want to *do* something."

"So what do you want to do? You can go back to school. I'll support us until you finish. We'll get by."

Cliff shook his head and looked at the porch floor. "I don't know what I want to do," he said. "If I stay with bodybuilding, I need a definite edge to make any real money, and I don't have that edge at the moment. I don't want to go back to porn either, but… what else is there?"

David breathed deeply. "Cliff, I need to ask you something I've been putting off for a while. Something that's been in the back of my head ever since we started inviting other guys into our lovemaking. Do we need therapy? Not just because of the basement ordeal. Do we need couples therapy?"

Cliff was silent for a few seconds, then leaned over and kissed David on the cheek. "We'll discuss it later." He rose. "I'm going to go get ready for the party."

David was still. What could he do? He sat for a moment more. There was no talking about it now. David didn't want to push things with Cliff. He would get cleaned up and head downtown to press charges against Nanna Hench.

THE two new nurses at St. Grey's Hope Memorial Hospital rode up the elevator together. They were bedecked in a similar fashion—old-timey white uniforms complete with folded white hats that sat snugly on their heads—but anyone could see the tall black nurse was the one in charge. She just had that look of class and authority. The look that said, "You *will* take your meds, Mr. McMurphy!" And aside from her more regal bearing, she *had* won the argument over who was to be in charge. Coin tosses were indisputable. Terrence, of course, had put up a protest anyway, but Vera wouldn't hear it.

"I'm the boss, applesauce!" she had snapped on the drive over to the hospital. "Besides, that blonde wig you're wearing looks as ratty as my Aunt Catalina's, and there ain't nobody who's gonna be fooled that you're a man anyway. Just look at all that makeup you got piled on your face. This ain't Vegas."

Terrence, ready to pop, held his tongue until they were in the elevator. He had been trying to think of something witty to say, but as the elevator door had closed, he touched up his golden wig and blurted out, "You look like a hooker. Like a big ol' hooker."

"You better watch yourself, Nurse Ratched!"

"Or what? What will you do, Florence?"

But the doors slid open and the ladies emerged from the elevator with style and decorum.

"What's the name of that doctor you're seeing, Vera?" Terrence asked loudly, stationing himself by the elevator. "You know. The plastic surgeon who fixed you up so pretty. What's his name again?" And then, to a passing family, Terrence said, as if giving them needed information, "She's a whore, you see."

Vera simply raised her hand in indifference as she walked on to Becky's room, her heels *clack-clack-clacking* on the floor. Terrence stayed, satisfied with his victory, at the elevator. This was part of the plan. Operation Rescue Ridgeworth was underway.

Terrence looked at his reflection in the steel elevator door. "Stunning," he said.

Becky's eyes lit up full bloom when Vera entered her room pushing a wheelchair she had found in the hall. Nobody seemed to be using it, after all. Miss Lo sat quietly in a chair beside Becky's bed. Her eyes narrowed in suspicion. She looked Vera up and down and did nothing to try to hide the fact that she didn't like the look of her.

"Who you?" she asked. "I never seen you here before. What you want?"

Vera smiled broadly. "Why, I'm part of a new hospital nurse transfer program, my dear."

"I not heard of this."

"It's *brand* new."

Miss Lo watched closely as Vera pulled the wheelchair close to the bed.

"What hospital you from?" Miss Lo inquired.

"Oh, you know. That one," Vera said, stalling, as she helped Becky into the wheelchair.

"What hospital?" Miss Lo reiterated as she stood up.

"Listen, girl!" Vera became suddenly fierce. "You better get the hell out of my face. I got a job to do. They told me to come and get a Miss Becky Ridgeworth, and that's what I'm doing. I haven't got to answer to anyone but her. You hear me?"

169

She began wheeling Becky to the door, leaving Miss Lo shocked where she stood. Vera and Becky had just turned, smiling, into the hallway when another nurse—a big muckety-muck on the floor—passed them. She looked into the room at Miss Lo and said, "Who is that? And where is she taking Miss Ridgeworth?"

Vera, having overheard this, gave a shout of "Hold on to something, baby!" and hauled ass to the elevator. Miss Lo raced out of the room, going as fast as her little legs could carry her, screaming, "You hold on! You wait! You no nurse!"

Terrence was in the midst of flirting with an orderly when he saw Vera barreling toward him with Becky. He squealed and pounded on the elevator button. It opened just in time, blessedly vacant, and Vera pushed Becky in. Terrence followed.

"Isn't this exciting?" Becky exclaimed.

Miss Lo did not manage to reach the elevator in time, but did manage to shout, "You in big trouble now!" before the doors closed.

"Happy Halloween, baby," Vera said to Becky triumphantly.

They left the wheelchair in the elevator and ran to the car just in case Miss Lo was still after them. She looked like a rather relentless little woman, and they didn't care for her sort of grown-up foolishness. After all, it was Halloween, and there was so little time to get ready before the party. As they sped away in Miss Vera's car, they whooped it up and cheered like three outlaws, half expecting a pursuit by Johnny Law and a bit disappointed when it didn't happen.

AS EVENING fell, the monsters and the freaks came out on Jasper Lane. Some of them even wore masks. Others simply carried picket signs and shouted religious catchphrases that required neither wit nor proper spelling. These particular people were either ignored by everyone else intent on going to Cassie Bloom's party on the hill, or marveled at as a novelty. Despite this apathy shown her—or perhaps fueled by it—Nanna Hench drove about in a wide circle on her fancy new scooter below the Bloom residence, bellowing into a scratchy megaphone. The twenty or so people who had volunteered to support her righteous cause bobbed and weaved in the middle of her angry circle, their faces grimacing uglier than any of the masks worn to the party. Mr. Scott himself hid in the middle of the circle, showing his support for the cause while not necessarily showing his face. One needn't be conspicuous when supporting intolerance, after all. Anonymity could be a powerful tool.

The costumes worn by the partygoers lay at varying degrees of the inspiration spectrum.

Rick Cooper-Tucker had decided that he and James would get into the Halloween spirit this year. Neither had ever been a particularly staunch Halloweenist, but the peer pressure was too great. Rick searched all over town until he found a couple of dime costumes that a local bank had used in some terribly cheap and tacky television ads. Inspiration struck.

"We're a paradigm!" he said to James when he showed him the costumes. "Get it?"

James did not, but he went along with it anyway. He didn't actually "get it" until he looked up "paradigm" on the Internet. It warranted a smirk and a "Silly boy," if not a laugh. When they showed up at the party, they needed a wide berth.

David and Cliff received many a stare when they arrived at Cassie's as it didn't take much prep time. David wore a red velvet cape with a hood and tiny black briefs with the word "Basket" over his basket. Cliff wore a black leather thong with a tail extension. His ass completely gobbled up any sign of that leather thong in the back. He'd found his mask at a local theater department—a snarling wolf's head that fit completely over his own. They walked slowly—menacingly—past the picketers. The wolf looked at Nanna, as did Red. Oh, they gave her good long stares from beneath the hood and the mask. Enough to hush even her momentarily. Uncertain as to who they were, she quickly drove to the other side of the circle.

Terrence waited until the Mean Girls arrived at his house before they strutted up the street to Cassie's party, dressed as an evil cheer group. Harry was not able to attend the celebration with Terrence, which was fine. Things were still tense between them anyway. And this way Terrence could be as loose in the tongue as he wanted, maybe in more ways than one.

The picketers were, of course, distressed by the sight of the drag cheerleaders. They had heard about the cross as well as the unprovoked attack on Mr. Scott in his very own home. Terrence and the Mean Girls eyed the group as they passed, hands on their hips, beating back the hate launched at them with their own arched eyebrows and plenty of attitude.

"Take it slow, girls!" Terrence shouted to his crew. "Let them see some slo-mo shoulder-and-hip action."

And they did. It was a full five minutes before all the Mean Girls had passed by the circle.

Melinda kept her word, and she and Coach Nipple had their date that night. She suggested they get to know each other in the biblical sense... at the party, that was. There were numerous costume ideas in the Bible. After all, she explained to him, she was still a Christian. Malcolm thought it was a wonderful idea. Or that was what he told her. But then, he would have said anything was wonderful if it meant a date. Melinda was a serene Mother Mary (who else?). With a frown, she met Malcolm at her door. While his costume was biblical, it was only biblical-lite.

"What's wrong?" he asked with a grin as she opened her front door to him. He wore a beard, flip shades, and a white-and-gold robe that would only have been appropriate on Broadway. "I'm Jesus Tap-Dancing Christ." He did a little jig to prove his identity.

Melinda worried about getting through the picketers with such an obvious attempt at blasphemy, but they went unharassed.

"Bless you, my children," the coach said as they passed through. "Bless you. Fish sticks and wine for everyone!"

Melinda tried to suppress her snickers even as she told him to quit acting like a teenager.

Finally, on the deck of the Bloom home, Cassie herself made her grand entrance to the party. Her costume was part of a glittering threesome with Becky and Vera—the Supreme Witches of Eastwick. They were a tacky mixed homage to girl groups and Updike. Their hair was jacked to heaven and their necklines were cut as low as hell. There would even be a performance number later in the evening if they were all still standing. (Though, they all agreed, Becky was not to drink.)

Once Cassie had mingled a good fifteen minutes, the music was turned low. Cassie picked up a wine glass and tapped it on the side to gain attention. The crowd hushed as the hostess spoke.

"I'm so happy to see you all here," Cassie said. There was no microphone. Her voice carried well. "This has been such...."

But before she got very far at all, she was distracted. Using her megaphone, Nanna Hench had begun shouting up blasphemies at the hostess. "Jezebel!" she screamed. "Your sinful ways will not go unpunished!"

Her angry crew agreed in jeers.

Cassie's face, normally proud, seemed to lose a little focus. The crowd murmured.

"You're a terrible mother! Your son is lost! Lost to the flames of hell, and it's your fault!"

Cassie's face had fallen completely now. She simply stared down the hill. It was a look of shock. As if someone had told her Jason was dead. The words "terrible mother" hung in the air.

"Don't you listen to her, Cassie Bloom," Vera said, coming up beside her friend and taking her hand. "That woman hasn't gotten to you as long as we've known her. She's a mad little hypocrite. Don't let her bother you tonight."

Melinda was blushing with rage. She hadn't noticed that she was gripping the coach's hand too tightly until he said, "Ouch!"

"I hate that old woman," she seethed between gritted teeth.

Cassie continued to look down at the protestors. She seemed lost, not at all the woman everyone knew. Her face was wet with tears. The party seemed dead before it had even started. Awkward whispers filled the deck. A heaviness lay over everything.

And then there were headlights. Two sets of them, a van and a small car. Cassie's gaze shifted.

Nanna stopped ranting, and she and her picketers turned to determine the identity of the new arrivals. Were they friends or sinners? Either way, how dare they take away from Nanna's moment of vitriol and victory?

The van pulled to one side of the circle and came to a stop. The side door to the van slid open. The picketers who had worked at the gay aversion camp, Straight To The Heart, knew at once who these people were. These were sinners. Jason Bloom got out of the driver's seat, and he and his rescued clan of nine once again stood proud and ready for battle.

Up above, Cassie smiled broadly, her heart leaping. The heaviness in the air was at once lifted.

"There's your boy," Vera said as she hugged Cassie's shoulder.

The small car pulled up to the other side of the picketers' circle. It was a small maroon Festiva with five very large barbarian-clad bodybuilders inside. The five Conans squeezed out of the car until they all stood facing the now trembling picketers. Thumper looked ready to eat some purified meat. Barbarians didn't believe in this type of freedom of speech.

On the deck, Cliff took off his wolf's head to get a better look at what was going on below. "Well, I'll be!" he said with a smile.

Then, as if someone had shouted "Charge!", both groups—the teenagers and the barbarians—came at the picketers.

"Pound 'em!" came the 'roid-raging cry from Thumper. "Pound 'em!"

Pandemonium ensued as screaming picketers scattered. The barbarians came at them from one angle, the camp refugees from another, and, from atop the hill, some very gleeful gay drag queen cheerleaders.

"It's a trap! A trap!" Nanna cried as her scooter drove, momentarily stuck, in circles. She finally broke from her roundabout and set off to retreat from Jasper Lane when Jason Bloom stepped in front of her.

"Judas!" she yelled. "Move it, homo!"

She ran the scooter into his shins. He fell to the ground in pain, allowing Nanna another chance to get away.

"Oh, no, you don't!" Melinda had raced down the hill with Jesus and the drag queens. With Malcolm's help, she pulled the scooter back even as it protested.

"Are you okay?" Melinda asked Jason as the coach kept hold of the scooter.

"I'm fine," he answered, rising but rubbing his leg. "Thanks."

"Let go my chair!" Nanna yelled, swatting at the Christ.

"I forgive you, my child," Malcolm said with every swat, refusing to step out of character. He was struggling with the motorized beast *and* the beast that drove it.

"You're staying right here, Nanna!" Melinda yelled back.

Finally, Nanna got free and rose from the scooter. She tried to run. Melinda was right behind her, though, and took her down.

"Citizen's arrest!" Melinda called out as they both tumbled to the ground.

Nanna struggled and snarled like… well, like a badger.

"Ma'am," Coach said to Nanna, "you are going to need to calm down." He turned the scooter off.

Nanna, not having seen the coach's outfit until just then, cried out, "*Jesus Christ!*"

Coach Nipple smiled at her and did a little dance. "That's Jesus *Tap-Dancing* Christ," he clarified. "You need any help?" he asked Melinda as she lay atop Nanna Hench.

"I've got her," Melinda said.

"That's my girl," the coach replied with a wink.

175

The hysteria continued around them. There was a lot of screaming from the picketers, much cackling from the Mean Girls, and some very primitive growls from the barbarian horde. Thumper even stopped to pose for an audience of two admiring Mean Girls, but they were all soon back in the fun.

Coby and Seth, having decided to let Rick know they were no longer crushing on him, had driven to Jasper Lane and stood in front of Coby's Pinto, uncostumed, watching the goings-on with complete bewilderment.

"It's like a Cirque show," Seth observed.

A drag queen cheerleader with a toy pitchfork lawn ornament ran past them. She was chasing a woman whose own Halloween costume looked to be that of some kind of dull camp counselor.

"What's going on here?" Coby asked the queen.

"It's the apocalypse!" the queen answered with glee. "Join in!"

The plastic pitchfork was shoved into Coby's hand, and the queen resumed the chase after the counselor. Coby looked, puzzled, at the plastic pitchfork for a moment, and then, startled by a great roar from one of the barbarians, he turned quickly toward Seth.

"Fuck!" Seth shouted. "My eye!"

Up on Cassie Bloom's deck, those who weren't chasing picketers and flirting with barbarians watched the proceedings with drinks in hand. They were much entertained. With a limp, Jason made his way up the Halloween path to his mother. Cassie stood with Vera and Becky in the row of spectators. Cassie embraced her son and kissed him on the forehead.

"Did you get everything you needed accomplished?" she asked.

"I did, Mother," he said. He gestured broadly to the mayhem happening below. "Do you like what I brought back for you?"

Becky and Vera laughed wickedly at the circus below, encouraging laughter in those around them.

"It's the best coming home gift a mother could ask for."

UNSEEN, Mr. Scott had slipped away from the chaos. Almost. Gayhound, ever the neighborhood watchdog, saw him and took chase, nipping at Mr. Scott's heels all the way to the house where the old man had lived. Mr. Scott locked the door behind him and kept the lights out, hoping that the dog's barking outside was not attracting any attention.

He quickly made his way to the back door, humming an increasingly optimistic melody with each step. He always thought he had the most pleasing of voices, no matter what people like Nanna Hench said. As he placed his hand on the doorknob, however, he was suddenly jolted off guard by a slight movement in the corner.

"Who's there?" he said. "Who is that? Show yourself immediately! I will not suffer derelicts and degenerates in my presence."

Michelle came out of the shadows. She looked, in many ways, a totally different person. She had cut her hair short and neat and was wearing trendier clothing than she had in the past. By that vacant look in the eyes, though, Mr. Scott knew it was most certainly Michelle.

Mr. Scott smiled nervously. "My, my. You look lovely, sweet Michelle. Just—"

He reached out for her, and as he did so, she swung at him, and the knife she carried sliced through his arm.

Mr. Scott howled and fell backward, blood flowing freely all over the floor. Michelle came nearer to him with a more assured walk than he had ever seen her use.

"No," he pleaded. He raised the other hand to shield himself from any more blows. "No. We can start over. Just you and me. Help me stop the bleeding and we can begin again. We can start something brand-new, the two of us. Right here on Jasper Lane. Why, you can even be in charge? Would you like that? How would you like that?"

She stared at him blankly.

His demeanor suddenly changed. "Young lady, you put that knife down this minute! I found you when you were just a little helpless nothing covered in blood. A bloody runaway. I gave you a life!"

Nothing from her but steady breaths.

"Please don't," Mr. Scott began to beg, sliding in his own blood. "Please don't hurt me."

"Mr. Scott," Michelle finally said. He had never heard her speak before. It was a voice of shadows, of curving esses and apathetic breaths. She raised the knife. "I'm getting the hell out of this town and on to bigger things. This is what my real family couldn't understand either, this need of mine to be... different. Like you, they were easy to get rid of."

"No. I can be good for you. I can come with you."

"Yes, indeed," Michelle said. "You *are* coming with me, Mr. Scott. You and Sister Sally and Brother Newt are all coming with me."

Mr. Scott screamed for help as the blade came down on him again and again, but the pandemonium outside made sure his cries went unheard.

The Final Chapter

BUT for a few carousing barbarians and drunken slutty cheerleaders milling about on the street below, the Halloween party was over. Cassie saw the last party guests stumble away around four in the morning.

"Best party ever!" proclaimed the drag queen whom Terrence always referred to as Liza. Then she headed down the hill... rapidly. That is, poor Liza fell and kept rolling. At the bottom of the hill, she got up as if nothing had happened and staggered to Terrence's house, where most of the cheerleaders were staying over.

Cassie spent the next hour seeing to sleeping arrangements for her new guests from the camp. Straight from *that* heart and into hers. When that was done—when they were all fast asleep and free of worry—she and Jason took a look at the basement together.

They stood at the foot of the stairs, eyeing the long corridor that had been constructed for an appalling purpose. It was horrid and quiet down there. There was an air to the place that still gave Cassie the chills. But she supposed that would always be the case, no matter how it looked.

"I like this idea," Cassie said. "We're taking something so awful and turning it all the way around and inside out. We're not just masking it. We're transforming it. Your father would have been horrified."

"From a gay aversion clinic to a halfway house for gay youth." Jason smiled. It was the first authentic smile Cassie had seen on his face in some time. Maybe ever. "Poetic justice... or something like that."

"We definitely need to liven it up down here. Some new, more vibrant colors would help. And some lighting that doesn't remind one of an Eli Roth movie."

"The kids will be glad to help." Jason didn't seem to want to move any farther into the basement. Cassie realized he was just as uncomfortable with it as she. "We'll get started as soon as they wake up."

"Why not wait another day? Let's let everyone rest." She took his hand. "Including you. You've been through a lot."

"Thanks, Mother." Jason's eyes were suddenly very gentle. He didn't look as half-crazed as Cassie had feared he would. "I appreciate this more than you know."

"Anything for you, darling."

"I was worried—just a little—that you wouldn't want to do this."

Cassie frowned. "Why in heavens would you think that?"

"Skeletons," Jason said with a sly grin. "Skeletons in closets."

"You knew?" She couldn't play too surprised. "Well, we weren't able to recover… every bone."

"Don't worry about the skull, Mother," Jason said bluntly. "Dad and I took a little trip. He got all gussied up. And then he lost it—his head, I mean—in the Ohio River."

Cassie shivered. Her concern for Jason's mental state grew.

"Dark thoughts," she said, remembering what she had done with the rest of the bones. "This basement is filled with them. When we're cleaning this place out, Jason, that incinerator has got to go."

STILL in costume, Becky and David sat in Becky's living room. The television was on but nearly mute. David was wrapped up in his red hooded cape, and Becky laid her now flattened head of hair on his shoulder as they talked of serious matters over a special Halloween Hammer Film marathon.

"Has Cliff ever done this before?" Becky asked. She was unfazed by the gore on screen. "Has he ever decided to work out at such an odd hour?"

"Never," David answered. "He keeps to his routine unless forced to do otherwise. He's always been reliable that way. But tonight, it was strange. His whole mood had changed. I have never seen him as serious. He took the wolf head off and said—right there at the party—that he felt like a workout. A hard workout."

"Shred Headz?"

"Most likely."

"That place is disgusting."

"I was like, 'Cliff, it's three in the morning!' But he just shrugged and left." David paused. "I'm worried about him. About *us*."

"What do you mean? You don't think he'd actually leave you?"

"I don't know. I've never been this anxious about our relationship. I've never had cause to. We've had arguments and disagreements like every couple, but those have been easy to mend. This… this is something completely different. Neither of us did anything wrong. There's nothing to blame it on, but I feel like…."

There was a silence like a train of thought going nowhere.

"Look at what you've been through, David," Becky comforted. "You two just need time to heal. That's all."

"I think I might be losing him, Becky." David's voice cracked under the weight of the words. "I think it might have already happened."

Becky snuggled up to him. Neither said another word for a long while as they watched the television flicker violent reds and rivers of gore.

Becky's cell phone rang for the twentieth time that night. They both took in deep breaths, as if it was each of their first breath since they had gone quiet.

"You better get that," David said. "Your poor father needs to know you weren't kidnapped by raving drag queens."

"Does he?" Becky asked.

She rose and answered the call. "Hi, Daddy," she said, heading to the kitchen for some privacy. "Yes, I'm fine.... They were my friends.... No, it was not for Terrence's TV show, Daddy.... Yes. I'll get hold of Miss Lo tomorrow...."

David sat alone in front of the television. He pulled the cape tight around him, and beneath his hood, he began to cry.

MELINDA GOLD and her sister, Bethany, sat facing each other at the dining room table of Melinda's home, both nursing cups of coffee. It had been an adventurous, if humiliating, evening for Melinda. She had tackled Nanna Hench and, with Coach Nipple's help, had succeeded in bringing the protesting bitch back to the house. Nanna name-called and fought as Malcolm held tight to her shoulders. The old woman went quiet, however, when she saw Bethany waiting in Melinda's doorway. In fact, she was even more shocked to see her than Melinda was. Nanna was silent, if only for a brief moment.

The coach brought Nanna into the house and sat her down in the living room.

"The Lord commands thee to be still," Malcolm said.

"Jump her if she moves, Malcolm," said Melinda.

"What are you going to do with me?" Nanna asked.

"Something you've had coming for a while," said Bethany as she leaned against the room's doorframe in a sleek black dress.

"You little bitches!" Nanna squealed as Melinda dialed the police. "You ungrateful little bitches. You would do this to your own mother? You would send me to the pen?"

"*Miss* Hench," Bethany said, "we would put you in a cage if we could, you miserable old bag. I don't know of anyone you've ever been a mother to."

"Melinda!" Nanna protested. She tried on a new voice. Something attempting sentimentality. "Melinda, darling. You don't want to do this. Think of everything I've done for you. You're a strong, capable woman because of me."

Melinda paused and bit her lip. The phone was to her ear.

Bethany looked at her sister. "Think of Patrick," she said.

Nanna was in near hysterics when the police arrived and she heard the charges of kidnapping against her. She all but admitted everything in her ravings. It wasn't long before she was in the backseat of a squad car.

"We've been looking for her since this afternoon," one of the arresting officers told Melinda. "Apparently, your mother is a bit of a troublemaker."

"I don't know if she makes trouble as much as stirs it up," Melinda responded.

Nanna was screaming at Melinda, her face pressed against the window, as the squad car pulled away. Thank God, Melinda thought, there wasn't an audience to see this. Everyone was either passed out from the party or too drunk to care.

When the house was quiet once again, Coach Nipple took a rest on the couch. "I'll be in here if you need me," he said.

Melinda and Bethany headed to the dining room to discuss other matters. Bethany told Melinda everything she had uncovered about their true family from all of her searching.

"So," Melinda said, digesting the news, "our mother was a stripper."

"A burlesque dancer. Yes."

"Call it what you want. It's still stripping. Do they even have burlesque anymore?"

"They did when you and I were conceived."

"It wasn't *that* long ago, Bethany. We're not ancient." Melinda sat back in her chair. "So what about our father?"

"I haven't been able to track down anything on a father. I'm still looking."

"My Lord! Who knows if it's even the same man? We could only be half sisters."

Bethany did not try to dispute this. In fact, when they were growing up, it was often commented on how Melinda and Bethany in no way resembled each other. One was all sugar and spice, the other was all sour patches.

"I'm searching all over the place," Bethany said. "In the meantime, we should go visit her. We should try and get to know her."

"Or real mother?" Melinda seemed doubtful. "She's still alive?"

"Like you said, we're not ancient. Neither is she. I found her in a small town in Alabama. I followed her around for a bit. I even bumped into her at the grocery store just to see what sort of response I would get."

"And?"

Bethany looked thoughtful. "She was nice. She was very nice. She would have certainly been a better mother than the one who kidnapped us."

"I wonder if she looked for us," Melinda said, her eyes glazing over. "How did you find out we were kidnapped in the first place? Do you know how it happened?"

"A friend of our real mother found me. I know some of what happened. Give me more time to look into it and I'll be able to explain everything."

"What a mess." Melinda shook her head.

"There is one more thing, Melinda, and it might be a big deal. Especially for you."

Melinda tensed. "What's wrong?"

"Nothing's wrong. It's just… there's a bit more to our mother's story. You see, a few years after we were taken, she met a man and they had a baby boy together."

"We have a brother?"

"Our mother and this man were dirt poor and eventually gave the baby up for adoption. I'm told it was a very hard decision to make. It broke them up. The baby was adopted by a well-to-do family, went to a good college, and then eventually moved... here to Jasper Lane."

Melinda's mouth dropped. Her eyes were saucers. She knew who their brother was before Bethany even reached into her purse and pulled out the birth certificate.

"Terrence!" Melinda gasped. "*Fuck!*"

TERRENCE woke with a start. He had blacked out in the Halloween decorations that lined the walkway up to Cassie Bloom's house. He had been spooning one of the lawn zombies for a couple of hours.

He sat up, still drunk and very confused, and looked around. He dragged an arm across his mouth, wiping away drool and smearing makeup. His wig would never be the same. The night was quiet and still. This was not a comfort after the dream he had just had.

After rising to his feet, he stumbled down the hill and onto the street, the last of the Mean Girls to leave the party. This was a situation that felt vaguely familiar. After all, in college he had always been the last to leave the fraternity parties, though the walk back to his own dorm was definitely more riddled with embarrassment. Especially if he hadn't managed to hook up.

Terrence did not make it to his own home, though. Instead, he headed for that of Asha and Keiko. Only they could help him. Only they had the answers he needed.

He rang the doorbell. He rang it continuously until he heard movement from inside the house. Keiko answered the door, wiping at her eyes. She was dressed in an oversized FBI T-shirt.

"Terrence?" She squinted. "Is something wrong? You look awful."

"I just woke up with a zombie," Terrence replied. "I'm fine. I need your help, though. You're witches, right?"

"What?" She sensed right away he was still very drunk. "Terrence, it's five in the morning."

"But you are witches, right?"

"We're Wiccan. It's a faith."

Asha came to the door. "What the hell is going on?" she asked. "Is something wrong with Cliff or David?"

"No, no, no," Terrence said as if brushing the matter aside. "That's yesterday's news."

"He's on some religious survey or something," Keiko said. "He wants to know about Wicca."

"I don't care about Wicca!" Terrence exclaimed. "We need a séance. I need me some witches."

They looked at him and shook their heads, saying nothing.

"Look, I had a dream—"

"A hallucination?" Asha said.

"A dream. And in this dream I saw two ghosts, and I swear they were that mean woman and the little boy from the Jones's old place. You know, the Crazies!"

Still nothing from the ladies.

"Don't you see?" Terrence said. "They were murdered and have come back to haunt Jasper Lane. I don't want to live down the street from a couple of angry religious ghosts!"

In the middle of his explanation, his wig, having lost its spirit, fell to the ground.

"Terrence, honey," Keiko said, "call *Ghost Seekers*. We don't do séances. And aside from that, no actual bodies have been found. Now go home and sleep all that alcohol off."

Keiko leaned over and gave him a kiss on the cheek before closing the door. Terrence walked back toward his house. *Ghost*

Seekers. That was a reality show in which a team of sorta-scientists scoured old houses looking for spirits and demons and saying things like "What was that?" and "Did you hear that?"

"*Ghost Seekers,*" Terrence said aloud. It actually wasn't a bad idea. They would probably even bring in an exorcist to get rid of any evil Sally they came across.

"Yes," Terrence said as he looked defiantly at the Jones's old home. He held up a fist so as to give the moment needed heft. "You will haunt me no more, Sally of the Crazies! I'm gonna *Ghost Seek* the shit out of you."

CLIFF, now donning his gym wear over his wolf thong, waited in the locker room of Shred Headz with Thumper. Thumper still wore his barbarian ensemble from Cassie's party and most likely would wear it for the rest of the day. He liked how it looked on him. Cliff hadn't been drinking at the party and so was able to offer Thumper a ride to the gym. Thumper was still drunk, but he wasn't truly planning on doing any training. They were there for a different matter altogether. It was still so early in the morning that the gym had only two other patrons in the lifting area, and they were new.

"So," Cliff said as he sat on an old wooden locker room bench the color of mud, "you trust this guy's stuff?" The lights flickered overhead, in need of replacement.

"It's quality, man," Thumper answered. "This guy may look like a weasel, but he knows what he's doing. I've put on some surreal poundage since I started taking what I bought from Coby. Like cartoonish muscle. Don't be anxious, man. You'll see. You'll be ripped. Ripped!"

Thumper was so very loud—and extremely large—for a university professor.

Coby came rushing into the locker room as quick and darting as a mouse. He was noticeably excited. "Sorry I'm late," he said. "I was at the hospital when you called me, Thumper. I've got your stuff."

He put down his camouflage backpack on the bench and started quickly shuffling through it.

"Anything serious?" Thumper asked. "At the hospital, I mean?"

"My… boyfriend had a slight eye injury," Coby said.

"Jesus." Cliff shook his head. "Does everyone you get involved with have to lose an eye?"

Coby looked offended. "He's fine. He'll keep it. And *he's* forgiven me. He's all heart, this one. I mean, it was an accident, after all. If that ugly cheerleader hadn't handed me that pitchfork—"

"You got the stuff?" Thumper asked, now impatient.

Coby brought out two small white boxes, one for each bodybuilder. "The needle is in there, in case you need one."

Cliff eyed the box in his hands, not bothering to open it. He thought of David. *I'm doing this for you, baby.*

"You're gonna be pumped to smithereens, man!" Thumper encouraged him with a nudge.

Cliff retrieved his wallet from his locker and paid for the purchase. He showed some hesitation but went through with it. He was taking control. He was trying to be a better Cliff. No sooner had he done this, however, than he heard heavy footsteps rush up behind him.

Thumper said, "Shit!" and Coby's face went white as he raised both hands in surrender.

"You're all under arrest," said one of the two plainclothes officers who had been working out in the gym. "No sudden movements, big guy."

They took the small box from Cliff's hand, and Cliff bit his lip as he was put into handcuffs.

ERIC ARVIN resides in the same sleepy Indiana river town where he grew up. He graduated from Hanover College with a bachelor's degree in history and has lived, for brief periods, in Italy and Australia. He's survived brain surgery and his own loud-mouthed personal demons.

Visit his blog at http://daventryblue.blogspot.com/.

The SubSurdity Series

http://www.dreamspinnerpress.com

Romance from ERIC ARVIN

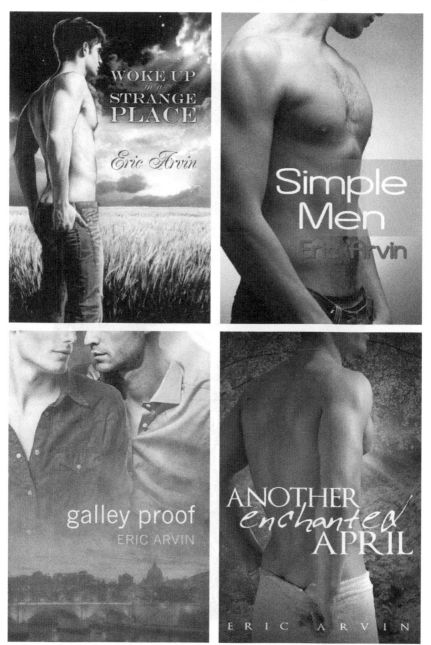

Lightning Source UK Ltd.
Milton Keynes UK
UKOW06f0028040816
279937UK00017B/602/P